Schlock! Webzine
Vol. 7, Issue 28

Edited by Gavin Chappell

Copyright © Schlock! Webzine 2015

This week's cover illustration is *Portrait of Tutankhamun's inner mummy case replica, taken at VAM Design Center, Budapest, during the Tutankhamun's Treasures exhibition* by HoremWeb. All images within licensed under Creative Commons Attribution-Share Alike 3.0 via Wikimedia Commons unless otherwise indicated. Graphic design © by Gavin Chappell, logo design © by C Priest Brumley.

All rights reserved. No part of this book may be reproduced or transmitted in any form or by any electronic or mechanical means, including photocopying, recording or by any information retrieval system, without the written permission of the publisher and author, except where permitted by law.

The right of Gavin Chappell, James Rhodes, Gary Murphy, Benjamin Welton, Gregory KH Bryant, and Rick McQuiston to be identified as the author of this work has been asserted by him in accordance with the Copyright, Designs and Patents Act 1988.

Published by Schlock! Publications 2015

ISBN-13: 978-1511631419
ISBN-10: 1511631414
This book is a work of fiction and any similarities to actual persons and/or places are purely coincidental.

Schlock! Publications
www.schlock.co.uk

CONTENTS

Editorial	I
Nobody Puts Graham In A Coffin....James Rhodes	7
Death Cop………………….………..Gary Murphy	24
It……………………….............Gregory KH Bryant	32
Death Comes in Kaleidoscope…...Benjamin Welton	35
Just The Right Addition…..………..Rick McQuiston	47
Terror On Snail Island……….…..Gregory KH Bryant	50
Retribution……………….….……...Gavin Chappell	66
The Jewel Of The Seven Stars………..Bram Stoker	72
A Connecticut Yankee In King Arthur's Court……………………………..……….Mark Twain	84

EDITORIAL

THIS WEEK Schlock! Webzine is celebrating four years as purveyors of the finest schlock horror, fantasy and science fiction. We begin with a story of a private investigator and his voyage to the bottom of the sea from first ever Schlock contributor James Rhodes, author of *The Hettford Witch Hunt* series and short story *This Is What's Happening*, followed by a post-apocalyptic superhero tale from Gary Murphy. Next we have a new horror tale from Gregory KH Bryant, whose B-Movie horror epic *Terror on Snail Island* reaches Part Eleven elsewhere in the zine, followed by *Death Comes in Kaleidoscope* from Benjamin Welton.

We also see a horrific return from Rick McQuiston, while I've included the first story I wrote, back when I was fifteen and being thirty four was far ahead, not behind me (previously featured in issue 3). We also begin a new serial, *The Jewel of the Seven Stars* by Bram Stoker, adapted by Hammer Horror in the seventies as *Blood from the Mummy's Tomb*. And in chapter two of *A*

Connecticut Yankee at King Arthur's Court, our hero encounters a page.

Meanwhile if you happen to be in the North West of England, and would like a chance to meet horror author Ramsey Campbell, among others, (including your 'umble editor), why not come down to the Wirral History, Mystery, Music, Mind, Body and Soul Fair on 23rd May? Tickets now available (only £4 for adults, £2 for senior citizens) from http://www.eventbrite.co.uk/e/wirral-history-mystery-music-mind-body-and-soul-fair-tickets-15861251430. That's right; only four whole English pounds to meet the Master of Horror, the man S. T. Joshi called 'the leading horror writer of our generation, every bit the equal of Lovecraft or Blackwood,' Ramsey Campbell himself! Roll up, roll up! Bargain, or what?

-Gavin Chappell.

Rogue Planet Press: Submissions Call

Harold S Delay—Red Nails I

Swords against Cthulhu
Deadline: June 1st, 2015
Payment: Exposure and Royalties
Short Stories—up to 7, 500 words

Swords against Cthulhu, an anthology of sword and sorcery/Cthulhu Mythos crossovers: mighty thewed barbarians battle against alien wizardry and cosmic terror in a blind, unreasoning universe where only the strong survive...

The Cthulhu Mythos is best known as a horror genre, but its influence was felt on the work of seminal sword and sorcery writers Robert E Howard and Clark Ashton Smith, and its pessimistic tone has continued to predominate in the genre to this day. However mighty the hero, the forces of chaos, the blasphemous powers of an insouciant universe, are stronger—or are they? All a doomed swordsman can do is face the outer darkness, blade in hand, a song of defiance on his lips, and hope to die fighting…

Sword and sorcery, sword and soul, dark fantasy, and sword and planet stories featuring mighty warriors and rogues pitted against the horrors of the Cthulhu Mythos will be welcome in this anthology.

Submission guidelines:

Please submit your manuscript as a *.rtf, *.doc or *.docx file (all other formats will automatically be rejected. Contact me prior to submitting if this presents an issue for you.)

Font and formatting: Please submit in Times New Roman, 12 point font; single line spacing. Please format the document to 1st line indentation of 1". The page margin should be set to .1" on all sides.

No headers, footers or page numbers.

Please check grammar.

Upon acceptance into the anthology, we ask that Rogue Planet Press holds exclusive publishing rights for six months from the date of publication; after that date has passed, all intellectual property rights revert to the author with the proviso that Rogue Planet Press retains distribution rights in the format of the contracted anthology.

This title will be available as an e-book and trade quality paperback.

Gavin Chappell will be presiding over this

anthology.

Email your submission as an attachment to: editor@schlock.co.uk

The email subject line must read 'SUBMISSION—Swords against Cthulhu– 'your story title" or your submission will not be considered for this anthology.

Successful applicants will be notified before the deadline has expired.

Edited by Gavin Chappell

NOBODY PUTS GRAHAM IN A COFFIN
JAMES RHODES

I watched the sunlight narrowing without the power to so much as raise my legs in resistance. The feel of velvet against my back felt glorious. I can honestly never remember such a sensation of total and complete serenity. Even when the lid to the coffin closed fully and I began to hear the hammering that would fasten me forever in a state of what the Catholics call perpetual rest.

One of the priests was talking over the coffin. I can believe the fuckers were actually giving me funereal rights when they knew damn well I was alive, if not necessarily kicking. I'm not sure if it was the effect of the drugs or the sheer bloody darkness. As my eyes struggled to adjust to the lack of light I swore I could see the face of my niece crying. Her dark skin shone in the darkness, her slender face stretched into an expression of forgiveness and acceptance that I had never known in life. It was my sins that had led to this, my actions. And Maria forgave me.

'Maria.'

The voice sounded in my head but I could not bring it

to my lips. Whatever it was that had been injected into me had done a number on me. I felt the dizzying slide of motion sickness crashing into a breathless finality. For a split second I was aware that I had been cast into the Atlantic before my consciousness became as dark as my coffin.

WHEN I began to dream, it was of Maria crying. I wasn't sure if she was crying because I was dead or because of the events that had led to me being drugged and cast into the sea. I felt the drip of her salt tears trickling over my cheeks and for a moment I couldn't tell if she was really crying or if I were weeping myself. I lifted my hand to wipe my cheeks clean and felt it bang against the lid of the coffin. With the ability to move returning, I realised that the water was not tears but seawater. From the constancy of motion I knew I was still floating in the wooden box. I pushed upwards with both hands and feet and felt the nails loosen. Encouraged by the sense of reprieve, I pushed again. Again there was the slightest give in the nails. Determined to get out of the box and to use it as a raft, I inhaled and threw every ounce of strength into the effort to open the coffin lid.

At the exact moment that I shifted all my bodyweight into the effort of escape, a wave caught the side of the box and I capsized. My nose broke as it smashed into the oak lid of what I assumed was to be my final resting place. I didn't have time to register the pain before the horrible sting of gelid water struck my skin. I felt the box upend with the weight of the accumulating water. Then the pull of gravity sank the box and its tender contents. In sheer blind panic I pushed. I have bench-pressed as much as 140 kilograms in the gym but the strength of my arms was no match for wood and iron. I took the last breath of available air in the box and closed my eyes. The pressure on my lungs was insurmountable. I remembered Maria's face and my sober mind pieced together the last few moments of my waking life:

It was my brother who had hired me to find Maria, which in real terms meant that I was doing the job for love. I was not much of a detective but I had a way of persuading people to tell me what they knew. My approach had always worked well when dealing with street gangs and nonces. I had found more than twenty lost children in the last decade and I always felt that anything else I had done was cancelled out by that good. The protection of the innocence of others, that was my code. Anyone I didn't consider innocent was pretty much fair game. With Maria there was the additional element that someone had messed with my family. From the beginning I had anticipated that it was going to be a brutal affair. I was going to enjoy myself, let a few of the krypteian urges in my head out of their chains. The church of Everlasting Peace didn't know what it had coming. Religion is just a gang that uses words instead of guns and low self-esteem instead of narcotics. I always said it and I always meant it. However, when it came down to it, they couldn't have been more different to a criminal gang.

For a start, the fuckers were organised. I have never come across such an organised state of total psychopathy. Each member was committed to their orders: they didn't question them, they didn't resent the lowliness of their tasks and they didn't expect anything back from them. How are you supposed to reason with people like that? What's worse is because everything was 'sacred' to the brainwashed morons, none of them ever asked any questions. The priest told them to guard a door and they guarded it, he told them they were all getting on a ship and they all got on it. None of them knew why and none of them cared why. Normally when you grab a man by the hair with your left hand and pull off his ear with your right hand, it tends to get him thinking over every single detail of the subject in question. But not in this case.

All members of the Church of Everlasting Peace wear

red robes like cardinals. They have similar hats too, and they have no authority structure that I have been able to discern. None of them will talk, not even to say who their boss is. Hurting them is like giving them a gift, instant credit with whatever the fuck it is that they believe in.

I should state for those of you that don't know, that I'm not being ignorant about the beliefs of the Church of Everlasting Peace, nobody knows. The church has around 700 members in England and nobody knows what they believe in or what they do all day. Nobody can call them a cult because aside from the word 'church' they show no religious activity at all; as a matter of fact they show no activity of any kind. They don't recruit, they don't have masses, they don't live on secret farms. The Church of Everlasting Peace pays rent for all of its members in private accommodation—they also pay what you might call a living allowance. People are lining up to join them but they don't take new members. Nonetheless, there are new members cropping up all over the country. One day they put on their red robes and just leave home. Where they get the robes is as much of a mystery as how they sign up.

When Maria disappeared, I hurt every member of the Church I could lay my hands on, but none of the bastards would say a word. Finally, I ran some facial recognition software that technically belonged to the London Metropolitan CID. I found one hit of Maria getting off a train in Portsmouth dressed all in red and wearing the signature broad-brimmed galero hat. The CCTV only caught her face because she happened to take off the hat and stare directly towards it. I didn't know what she was looking at but I suspected it was a deliberate attempt at being seen. Her eyes locked on the camera and she smiled, her narrow face filled with a sense of joy that mundane sanity doesn't offer.

I waited outside of Portsmouth station for days in the hope that I might catch another church member or that, better yet, Maria might make a return journey. On the third day, I spotted the red robes and stupid hat. I jumped out of my car and circled into the rush hour crowd. Approaching the everlasting bastard from behind, I gave him a quick shove in the right direction and had him in the back of the car before he knew what was happening. He put up no resistance, his acceptance was sanguine and compliant. He sat in the back with his hands on his knees. As I stepped into the car, he spoke in a quiet tone.

'The sea awaits us, brother.'

That was how I found the boat. I stepped onto it wearing the robes of the compliant church member. He didn't put up a struggle. I asked for the robes and he gave them to me. I kicked him out of my car outside of a charity shop and slipped him a fiver to buy some proper clothes. Down at the harbour it wasn't hard to spot a boat crewed entirely by people in red robes.

'You're just in time,' one of them said. The boat weighed anchor and set off the very instant my feet touched the deck. I waited till we were in international waters and then I started asking questions. Those bastards let me think I was outsmarting them.

THE WEIGHT of the coffin dragged it towards the depths of the North Atlantic and I held my breath so hard that I felt my lungs might explode with the pressure. As my hands flailed upwards, reaching desperately for a surface I couldn't possibly grasp, I felt a tiny pocket of air. I let the burning carbon dioxide free and with both hands putting pressure on the sides of the coffin I forced my head up towards the last available air. There must have been two inches of air at the top of the coffin. I managed to breathe in and out three times in quick succession, then as I took one last long breath and thanked the fates for giving me an extra few minutes of life, the coffin dropped.

Now when I say it dropped, I don't mean it sank deeper. The coffin began to plummet through open air. It was a repeat of the sensation I had had when I was first dropped off the ship. Except that the drop was longer and the impact was harder. The coffin landed on its back and the soft velvet might have cushioned the collision if it wasn't for Newtonian physics. I bounced up with the impact and smashed against the splintering lid. As the water drained out of the shattered oak, I took huge lungfuls of air. I kicked off the coffin lid and took a look at my surroundings.

The fall I had taken was not as dramatic as it had felt when I couldn't see it. I was stood on a rocky seaweed covered beach and about twenty feet above my head, suspended by some kind of viscous bubble, was the North Atlantic Ocean. There was only a thin twilight to illuminate the scene but what was around me was the canopy of ocean. I could not see how far it stretched but my first instinct was to walk in a straight line to touch the walls of the bubble. However, the intense cold gave me pragmatism. I stripped the red robes off my skin and rubbed my kidneys with the backs of my fists until my shivering petered out into a manageable shake rather than an all-consuming spasm.

Most men in my line of work, you can call us interrogative detectives, come to it after leaving the military and finding that civilian life doesn't really care how efficiently you can dispatch your enemies. I was a boxer, the type that wins all his fights and who promoters don't want their golden boys up against. After ten years of training I had nothing to show for my efforts but a right hook that could floor Hercules. I was a slender light heavyweight but could drop as low as middleweight when needed. The need became less and less frequent.

When a friend of mine asked if I could do a favour for him, I investigated the curious case of when exactly his business associate intended to pay the money he owed. It was the start of a lucrative career for me. I found out the reason I was so good at fighting is because I really do enjoy hurting people. It has to be men, that's my only rule. There's no satisfaction in beating a woman. I don't have anything against it per se, it just doesn't sit well on me.

With the Church of Everlasting Peace, my only-men policy caused me a few problems. About 75% of the people on the boat were women and about 10% of the men were frail and fragile enough to pass for women when they were wearing long red robes and broad brimmed red hats. It took me a good hour to find a man who could be persuaded into isolation. I saw a man mopping the deck and told him I had been asked to help. I got him to show me where the mops were stored. Half an hour later I had an ear in my hand and no information. I confess that I got a little frustrated with him. He was a block of lard and muscle, sat in a utility cupboard full of potential weapons, and all he could do was thank me for my 'purification.' When I had run out of fingers to break he still couldn't tell me where Maria was, or even who might know. He just kept on thanking me until I kicked him in the throat and waited for him to turn blue.

The boat was a large tanker, of the sort used for hauling freight containers: a huge steel block of utilitarianism full to the brim with people. I closed the door to the utility room, stepped out into a steel corridor painted in flaking white paint and immediately walked into a woman.

'Excuse me, have you seen Maria?' I asked.

The woman put a finger to her lip and walked past me as if I didn't exist. The stairs were made with latticed grates and my boots made no sound on them. At the bottom of the steps was a steel door set in a steel wall. The whole ship was a triumph of Spartan sensibility. I liked it. I pulled down the heavy handle and stepped into the room. There in front of me stood Maria. She stood next to a thin man with a curling pencil moustache. His smile was as ugly as a razor cut.

'Hello, Graham,' he said. 'Nice to have you on board.'

It was more or less at that point that someone stepped out from behind the door and jammed a needle into my arse. The last thing I can recall before blacking out is pulling the syringe out of my posterior and swinging it in the effort to slice a jugular. I could see the vein clearly but nothing else made sense to me. I heard a voice, Maria's voice, saying, 'I forgive you.'

But I digress.

I stood on the cold beach shivering like a toddler with hypothermia and wished to Christ I had any kind of survival training. I fell upon the ridiculous idea of taking some of the fragments of the oak coffin and rubbing them together to make a fire. There was one large splinter on the sand. I opened the coffin lid to see if there was any more inside. I saw it at the bottom of the coffin: Where my feet had been resting was a clear plastic zip-lock bag. I could see more of the stupid red robes. I tore open the plastic and pulled them out. I didn't hesitate to pull the fresh robes over my skin. As I unfolded the robe, some other items dropped to the floor. I let them fall in my hurry for warmth. The rough fabric tore at my skin as I dragged it over the salt and wet.

I turned my eyes to the fallen objects. There was a sliver square of material. I sat down to examine it, the material folded out into a blanket. I wrapped it around my shoulders and the warmth was appreciable. I can't say how long I sat there on the beach for but I didn't look at the other items until I only felt cold. There was a pack of five chocolate bars, generic versions of a popular glucose and caramel bar that bore the name Racer, and a small bottle of water. I reached for the chocolate first but found I couldn't swallow it without the help of the water. After eating I felt almost normal and examined the other objects.

There was a miner's light with an adjustable elastic strap. I couldn't be bothered fiddling with it just then or thinking about why I had been provided with any of the stuff, I just picked up the last item. Two sets of knuckledusters, held together by a thin plastic tie. I snapped them apart and slipped my fingers between the grips. With both hands turned into lethal weapons, my stomach turning chocolate into heat and the thermal blanket wrapped around me, I could only think of one course of action. I fell asleep.

I WOKE soon after and ate the last of the chocolate. I fiddled with the strap of the miner's light and secured it on the top of my head. I had sand in my hair and my skin was still chafed from the salt and water. It wasn't a pleasant sensation but I'd had enough of the dark to last me indefinitely. If I was going to find a way of getting back to Maria, I was going to have to work out where I was and how to get out home. I clicked the light switch to the 'on' position.

The thin light cast its line across the alien dusk of the beach. The only visible landmark was an outcrop of rocks next to which grew the most peculiar looking tree I had ever seen. It was more of a plant than a tree. Its trunk led seamlessly into its broad leaves. I scaled a high dune to get to it. My legs made slow progress treading into the soft dry sand. I'm not ashamed to say that I crawled before I reached the top; my hands punched deep enough to provide some traction.

The tree was as fleshy as a shaved cow, a mess of brown spots on a yellow canvas. I regretted drinking all my water. Now that I had my faculties, the obvious peril of my situation kept jumping out at me. I was stranded on a desert island that couldn't possibly exist and if I didn't find water soon I would be sure to die there. I wondered why my life had been spared from drowning, only to starve to death in landscape as foreign to me as the dunes of Mars or the smooth ice of Europa. I turned off my miner's light in the effort to preserve the one resource I had left.

I sat with my back against the tree, bemoaning the hopelessness of the situation in which I found myself.

Looking up, I noticed that the bubble of the ocean was only a few feet above the tree. I can't say exactly why, but I had an overwhelming urge to touch the material that bound me to the alien beach. Standing, I straddled the trunk of the plant. It had more give in it than I would have preferred. With some effort I shinned my way up the branch, until I reached a point where the leaves separated from the body. Whereupon I pulled myself up to the highest point that could hold my weight. The plant was not as sturdy as a real tree and I could feel it swaying beneath me. I reached up, my fingertips cooled as they stretched at the ocean. I couldn't quite reach the barrier. I strained myself to push the extra few centimetres but to no avail. The plant began to sway dangerously. I clung to the branch and waited for the plant to settle. I realised I was on the most elevated point on the beach and used my position to look around. I had been so busy trying to reach the sky that I had missed what lay below me.

The sand dune that I had just scaled had obscured the valley; it sat like a lake of dark water. It would be a long walk to reach it. But, I thought, what else did I have to do?

I won't bore you by describing the journey, the plodding steps over cold sand, the fatigue in my legs, the hopelessness of it all. Suffice it to say that it was a long time before I got to the valley and the journey was a grind. I had plenty of time to reflect on what was happening and to question whether or not my niece knew I was coming, whether or not my brother knew where I'd end up and whether or not I'd drowned and this was hell.

As I approached the valley, the sand became warmer underfoot. I still had my boots but as they were wringing wet, I had tied the shoelaces together and thrown them over my shoulder. I may not have much in the way of survival skills but even I know that you don't throw your shoes away unless you have a box with new shoes in it. The lip of the valley rose out of sight as I neared it, and I prepared myself for another uphill slog on a sand dune.

Again, I won't repeat the details of how I got up the dune, it was like getting up to the tree, except longer and even more tiring. I reached the top, gripped the rocks that the sand had settled against and pulled myself up.

Any breath that I had left was taken away by the view. The valley was a mass of the yellow trees and dark algae-covered rocks, and it was temperate; a warm house on a winter's day. I could feel the heat rising over my face. The thickness of the foliage was as intense as any forest I have seen on land and the flora as varied. I flipped the switch on my miner's light and made tentative steps into those wary Neptunian groves.

The array of colours that the miner's light caught ahead of me was staggering. Rich purple leaves contrasted with the yellows and browns. An entire light spectrum of violet cast patterns on crinkled leaves. At every step I marvelled at the beauty of my surroundings. I bent over to feel the texture of the violet leaves. Cautiously I broke off the edge of one of them and chewed it. If I didn't get sick, I would try eating more.

A crash from behind me brought me to my feet. A menacing figure slashed out of the leaves. The sword he raised at me was made of a row of sharks' teeth wound into the shape of a weapon by the hemp-like seaweed. The man himself was armoured by the leaves of yellow with brown spots. Plates on his arms, chest and legs. His face was masked by the yellow material too. Only his eyes were visible. They reflected the miner's lamp like will-o-the-wisps.

He didn't waste time on challenging me, charging in a straight line. He was broad-shouldered and tall; I'd say he had a good three stone on me. However, he had obviously never seen the inside of a boxing ring in his life. I waited for him to get close, his right arm raised to strike me, and then I switched to a southpaw stance and sidestepped so that his guard was wide open. I felt the knuckleduster sink into the mask of seaweed that covered his face and I caught him with enough force to snap his head to the side. He changed the path of his sword and slashed it at my legs. I managed to step backwards and one of the teeth caught on the loose robes. I circled around three more steps and my assailant adapted his stance to follow me. He came fast and I backed all the way into one of the seaweed trees. He brought the sword hacking at my neck. I bobbed under its path and didn't stop to see it embed into the plant. I threw my whole body into a kidney punch and the man dropped to his knee.

The slight sense of triumph dissipated at the feel of the club smashing into my shin. He must have had it hanging behind him as backup weapon. I stood my ground and threw a 'one-two' combination directly into his head. I followed it with a left uppercut, catching him full in the face. The extra weight I had put on my front leg caused it to buckle in agony. I tumbled onto my side and grabbed my shin in agony.

The attacker pulled off his mask. His skin had all the hallmarks of never having seen the sun; he was almost Inuit in appearance, hair black and skin as pale as ivory. I had split his eyebrow with one of the punches and the blood was trickling into his eye. That said, he was in better shape than I was; my leg wasn't broken but from the way it was swelling I could tell there was at least a fracture. I struggled back on to my feet. Putting all my weight on my back foot, I put my hands up to defend myself. It was a futile gesture. Without footwork there was no way I could go toe to toe with the brute that stood before me.

The man lifted his club and said something in his native tongue. He spoke with open vowels and harsh consonants. I had no idea what he was saying but it sounded Scandinavian to my ears. He still had the club in his right hand. It was an impressive and bulky object, like a truncheon but thicker and longer. The club was crafted out of solid jade. It must have been worth a fortune. As it stood, it was going to cost me my life. Still, the man had his mask off now. If I could get him in the temples, I might just put him down. One clear hook was all I needed.

The big man took a step forward and then knelt down. At first I thought it was a part of his fighting style but then I noticed how he was holding the club. It rested in his upturned palms and he raised it forward, beckoning me to take it. I stepped towards him, biting my lip against the agony of footfall and took the club with my right hand. The weight was more than I could comfortably handle but I wasn't go to show weakness. Once I had hold of it, the man dropped his arms and held his head up. For a second I considered finishing him off and then I met his eyes. He was ready for the blow, he either had something up his sleeve or this was some cultural ritual that I couldn't grasp. Either way I let the club fall to my side and pushed against it to take the weight off my leg. 'Fuck it,' I thought and I sat down opposite him.

The man spoke again and with the words he stood, picked up his discarded sword and disappeared into the bush. When I was sure that he wasn't going to spring out with a new weapon and finish me off, I strapped the club to my injured leg with some of the leaves. The leaves were hard to break but one of the shark teeth had come loose during the attack and I was able to hack and shape a few of them to fit the purpose. I took a few handfuls of the violet leaves and chewed them as I resumed my descent.

I was hobbling now and shaking, not from cold but from the pain of stepping. The splint was providing some relief but I was slowly stumbling from one yellow tree to another. I couldn't find anything rigid enough to serve as a walking stick so I had to move in short bursts and rests. I hadn't gone too far before I heard rustling in the trees to the right side of me. If it was another one of the seaweed warriors I was in dire trouble. I heard rustling behind me, to the right of me and finally I saw a man blocking my route ahead. In his yellow armour, he was indistinguishable from the man I had fought. His three friends stepped out around me and I felt strong arms seize me and pull me to the ground. One of the men spoke in a stern voice. I got the impression he was telling me to stay still, not that I had much choice about that. I felt a net slide under and around me. Each of the four men shouldered one corner of the net, lifted me up and began to walk. Struck by the thought that they were going to eat me, I sank into a morbid gloom.

THE TRIBE fed me and wrapped my leg in wet seaweed. The people of the valley lived in a clearing in the midst of the forest, the men practiced fighting which they called 'imlad' and those women who didn't join in told them off for it or batted flirty eyes at the victorious. They weren't entirely vegetarian as they seemed to get fish from somewhere, but most of their diet consisted of seaweed. That said, none of them seemed too slender for it. They slept in the warm air and the young couples made love in the forest whilst the children played with balls and sticks. I couldn't work out a thing the people were saying but it was obvious that they meant me no harm. The man who had attacked me was named Goreth. It seemed we were friends now.

Goreth was always asking me to show the other men my uppercut and my knuckledusters. Goreth had made his own set out of carved bone and he kept asking me for tips. I guessed there must be another tribe in the forest somewhere that they liked to have a good scrap with. I was looking forward to joining in. In the passing of a few days I was ready to forget my old life and settle down. The women of the valley were as lean as lamb. As soon as I worked out which women were available, I was happy to take any one of them and start on making a few children. Until then I planned to sit amidst the smoky lamps of the clearing and bask in the innocence of the place. The natives called the place Difrin Gwodel but I had taken to calling it Eden 2. I cast aside the terrible red robes and donned the costume of a native, a seaweed kilt. I had no worries except in sleep.

Whenever I slept I dreamed of Maria, I dreamed she was asking me questions. Was I happy? Did the people hurt me? Did I fight any of them? Did I know that she forgave me? I would wake screaming and with tears on my cheeks and the old women on the valley would bring me fresh water and rub my shoulders. I had the same dream for three days and when on the fourth day I woke refreshed from an empty formless sleep, I smiled for the delight of freedom.

Goreth grabbed my arm and pulled me out of bed, pressing my knuckledusters into my hands. As I stood, every ounce of joy fell from my body. The Church of Everlasting Peace had come to ruin my life afresh. The red robed freaks lined the perimeter of the clearing, each of them holding a glow-stick for illumination. The people of the valley had formed into groups. The men held shark-toothed swords and stood in a perimeter around the women and children, all except for Goreth who was leading me by the arm. We got to a point in the centre of the clearing. There stood two red robed figures. I recognised Maria immediately.

'What's going on?' I demanded.

'We have to thank you for serving as our scout.'

The man with the razor-cut smile grinned with serene smugness.

'You put me in a fucking coffin and threw me into the sea,' I rebuffed.

'You pulled Nathan's ear off and left him for dead.' Maria's voice was not reproachful; it had the patronising ring of a primary school teacher.

'Yes, because you went missing. How do you think your parents feel about you gallivanting around in some undersea kingdom?'

The question sounded better in my head than it did spoken aloud. Razor-man spoke again.

'We formed our church out of the spiritually aware. Only those adept at leaving their bodies could find our masses and only we who can travel anywhere know of this place.'

'Do you know what astral projection is?' asked Maria.

'Do you know what common fucking courtesy is?'

'All of our families have been contacted and told that we are safe and have moved away to live in eternal peace. We will visit them in dreams as often as they like.' Maria sounded confident in her insanity.

'So why put me in a coffin and drop me in the ocean?'

'We cannot enter the minds of these people,' said Razor Man. 'We needed a test subject to see how they'd respond. You have been dreaming of Maria since you got here, no?'

'Fuck,' I said. 'How could you, Maria?'

Maria held out her arms and the red robes dripped off them.

'Everlasting peace,' she cooed. 'We needed you because you are the best fighter any of us knows of. We needed someone who could deal with any hostility so that we could come here in peace.'

'Where are you going to live?'

'Right here,' said the razor man.

'How will I get back home?' I asked him.

'There is no way back that we know of. We have come to live in everlasting peace.'

I looked around at the valley people. The proud faces of the men stared without fear at the religious nutters. The bright-eyed women pushed curious children behind them. I knew in my heart that the last thing any of those people needed was a bloody church group.

'Go live up on the sand,' I told him.

'We need the clearing, we need the people to help us learn how to live here.'

'I'm not sure these people want everlasting peace,' I told him. 'They have innocence and happiness.'

'Our peace will not affect them.'

'So you are willing to adapt to their customs?' I asked him.

The razor man nodded.

'Of course,' he said.

'Brilliant. Put these on.'

I tossed him my knuckledusters. The razor man looked confused.

'I have no need for such things,' he told me.

'Oh yes you do,' I told him.

I pointed at the razor man.

'Goreth, imlad,' I said.

Goreth stepped forward with his fists raised. I had a feeling that the Church of Everlasting Peace was going to have a hard time adjusting to life in the valley, but I fucking love it here.

THE END.

DEATH COP
GARY MURPHY

BEAU CRIPPLER examined his Electro Eliminator's double-barrels and snorted as he pulled the black and indigo leather mask over his disfigured face to cover the wounds subject to him by the team of misfits he'd just heard were speeding up Highway 19 after committing a home invasion and ugly double-murder.

He lived in post-Apocalyptic Britain, and since the nukes struck five years ago, if the fallout hadn't fried your innards, the radioactive plethora of waste and its clogging aftereffects certainly wouldn't take long to grip your heart and squeeze it dry.

Crippler had survived the attack—and somehow, still, it had worked to his advantage, in that since he was Blood Group U (Unknown), the radioactivity had blended with his bloodstream, and after terrible convulsions and agonizing pain, had given him noticeable changes and transformed him not only physically for the greater good, but after much struggle, the revelation was he could actually fly and take to the skies at will.

His life was death…and he was the Death Cop, since

now the world was full of death, decay and multifarious acts of rape, murder and thievery amongst those who survived the massive global assault. Crippler had been a cop most of his life and would continue being so until the day he died…and because he was now superhuman, his dying was negotiable, because he had ailed very little since the attacks, and he currently felt strong and utterly invincible—and all he wanted to do—and always had—was be a good cop and serve the community in West Cumbria where he lived and slept in the Constabulary in the small rural town of Cleator Moor.

Keaton was at loose in the area.

The man who had previously tossed from his mind the botched robbery when Crippler arrived on the scene to rescue the hostages and ensure their general safety and release from the terrible situation, had sprayed the cop with gunfire, whereupon most of the oncoming shell pierced Crippler and ripped through the flesh layering his face. He had been thrown backwards and believed to be dead, as the gang jumped on motorcycles and fled the scene—carrying a cash reward hardly worth much—as banking systems dropped and people invested elsewhere, and since there was nowhere to spend the money they stole, for the world was in a deep financial ruin, as it recovered from nuclear devastation and battled the onset of human extinction.

But some cop, somewhere, issued across the radio that they were speeding up Highway 19 near the old disused hamlet of Workington Town, and travelling at an almighty urgent speed—later, as the same cop reported, because they had brutally butchered a young couple and needed to get the hell away from the crime scene ASAP…

'Keaton…' the Death Cop murmured under his breath as he departed the station-house near the Town Square, '…I knew this day would come, creep.'

However, by a sick twist of fate—which probably affected many others (many who didn't realize)—Keaton was also Blood Group U, and like Beau Crippler, had harnessed his new powers—and although he never had the ability of flight, had other crazy stuff he could do different to just mere humans.

As ever, Crippler observed the waste-lands below as he traversed the sky, as he travelled towards the place in Workington where the felon Keaton had been spotted, probably no longer on the road but deep in hiding somewhere counting his gathered stolen quarry. In a crumbling, dishonest world where crime ranked highly, for many it was the only route to venture along, otherwise there was nothing.

It was a triple-murder, in fact, where a senior was mowed down on a side-road by the escaping criminals as they fought to get out of view…but the helicopter presence in the sky had Keaton and his cronies nailed. Like lost sheep, Keaton and two other men had skid off the road and directly into a grass ditch. As Crippler arrived, they stood stranded in a vast field…looking upwards at the copter in the sky and gesturing defiantly and rudely. Even then they believed they were above the law.

When Crippler hovered overhead in a circling motion to get a full idea of the situation below, Keaton appeared aghast when Death Cop lowered himself until the abrupt time came to pass when Crippler stood there right before them. Only, Keaton wasn't afraid…

Far from it…he was arrogant and foolhardy as he said, 'You think I'm going to run away from a flying cop just because he shakes my arse over some poor innocents getting to meet their maker prematurely? It's what the Lord would have wanted…'

Crippler unmasked himself.

Keaton gasped, 'Ah, copper…yeah, I remember you. But if you seek revenge, I'm here to scupper any plans you might have in apprehending the dude that disfigured you…but, let's face it—you were not exactly an oil painting to start with, were you?'

'I'm taking you with me…preferably dead. Make my day…'

Keaton enquired, 'You have superhuman powers, eh? Well, let me tell you, boss man…so do I, my friend.'

'I'm not your friend, you insect. Dead insect…'

Keaton laughed and mocked. 'Really…?' He tossed his head back and laughed more, finally settling down to add in mock-petulance, '…I think you're sadly mistaken. I was born in West Cumbria, and I always wanted to OWN West Cumbria…because it never gave me a thing. What I got, I had to take, because it was withheld…and every day that passes, I get ever-closer to my dream. I WILL own West Cumbria because I love West Cumbria and its people…even if some have to perish and die along the way. My dream will be realized, though, copper.'

'You're about to die, Keaton. Your sell-by date just expired today…time to clean you off the shelf.'

Keaton tilted his head and scrutinized the superhero in police garb.

He said, 'Man, you're so ugly…did I really do that?'

Angry, Crippler raised his Electro Eliminator and prepared to fire. Yet something far stranger than the inner-workings and complex circuitry the weapon concealed within its black metallic casing, it was of no use on Keaton…for suddenly, an emerald shell, or a force-field, manifest itself around the gifted criminal, and when Crippler let loose a round or two, the radioactive beam deflected and the hot streams flew elsewhere.

Crippler knew it wouldn't be easy and acted on Plan B…playing Keaton at his own game, which incorporated powers of a sensory nature. It would be a battle of wits…

As the other two felons dispersed, Keaton and Crippler engaged in psychic war.

The fiend in the field outstretched his right hand and formed a fist, as if clutching Crippler's innards and tugging on them, squeezing all life from them and rendering them useless. Death Cop creased when he felt his lungs getting heavier, as if they experienced great weight pulling them down into his stomach and abdomen. If it continued, he would die…so he had to act fast.

'You must fly away and save yourself, Beau…' Keaton said.

It was strange how Keaton knew his name.

'Never…' Death Cop hissed, as blood emerged on his lips.

'But you will die, Beau Crippler.'

Crippler choked back the red stuff, 'If I die killing you, so be it. Prepare yourself…'

Death Cop concentrated…and suddenly a wild scattering of blue flowing veins appeared throughout Keaton's face as he moaned and doubled-up in the high grass, collapsing to his knees and holding his stomach once it ruptured and filled with varied bodily juices, the bile, the blood, everything he had eaten and drank—it all seemed to heat-up and go crazy as Crippler went to work on the despicable fellow in the field.

Although, as Keaton knelt in the grass, it seemed police matters were not completely over just yet, for all of a sudden a luminous orange glow lit the whole place up, and as it boomed forth in quality hue, it brought with it sound, an enormous sound at that which had Crippler clutch his ears at the supersonic din emerging from beyond the emerald-green barrier. The entire vicinity seemed to curve and bend, and eventually distort, as the magnificent sound reverberated and everything into chaos. Passers-by looked around and clutched their ears to protect against the squealing racket, but unlike a resilient Crippler, they felt it most, falling to the ground whilst their ears, nose and mouth oozed blood.

Crippler arched his head to look upwards into the cruel nuclear skies, once sunny and bright and beautiful to stare at and fall in love with. Not anymore, especially as it was madmen no better than Keaton that demanded the missiles took flight and wipe out nation after nation. The current planet Earth—his planet Earth—was mostly waste and desert with only few survivors attempting to rebuild and organize a new generation. It somehow seemed like a 'holy endeavour' but something to be applauded—if anything, for courage and bravery in such hostile times. Keaton was just a full-on imbecilic hindrance…

But when Crippler looked up he witnessed something obscenely awesome hovering in the grey-black heavens.

Directly above the field they were in, a craft appeared, like a huge black spherical dinghy, and it seemed two alien-like creatures—an unrecognizable species—were extending a long, spindly tentacle to grasp Keaton and perhaps deliver him from his fate here on Planet Earth. Their shrivelled, monkey-like grey facial-features looked deformed and misshapen and their eyes were small and squinty, as they narrowed in contempt for futuristic cop Beau Crippler—self-appointed, self-titled Death Cop, as the name fit the person, who simply powered around his police duties in and around the county of Cumbria where he had lived all his life.

Rescued now, the agonized Keaton reached out and took the blue-skinned appendage, and within a moment of psychic wandering he was removed from the mental torture affecting not only his thought-process, but his body and limbs, the oxygen entering his lungs and getting to his brain, and yet mainly his eyes in their sockets which seemed to bulge and protrude on stalks in a sickening cartoon way. The aliens snatched him away and, with him on board, their strange ship flitted away, upwards towards a bigger ship in the distant skies.

Crippler had almost been killed.

The aliens, by saving Keaton, had saved him—and, Crippler had to admit, for a moment it felt great in his world of death and imminent extinction. But then, as he breathed and focused his vision best he could, he wanted to cry out angrily at the cruel loss of his police collar, and missing out on murdering the bastard who disfigured him in this grotesque fashion, not too many years before.

Crippler had been forced to roam life as an ugly, masked creature, hiding…hiding behind the mask.

From his crouched position in the deserted field, surrounded by fields of dirt and dry dust, he watched as the same dirt and dust blew in the mild breeze and realized the world hadn't long now before becoming a completely dead planet. It was sad and unfortunate…but, you must fully accept the facts he thought, the world has given up on itself and there is no return to glory for its sick, mutated and dying societies and scarce civilian population, dotted across the maps featured in every atlas.

He watched the mother-ship drift off slowly at cruise-speed and fade into the horizon—and in an unexpected burst of blinding light, and a salad of multi-coloured rays, it charged off and vanished utterly. Crippler felt defeated and damned…a failure…useless…he would die alongside everyone else, feeling like this for the rest of his days, useless and dying.

But here, he felt the warm and soft hand touch his shoulder and he tilted his head to face the source.

A fresh-faced and beautiful woman looked down upon Crippler, yet obviously alien. 'I come to take you with me, my friend. Your nemesis has fallen into disruptive hands, and together with our enemies will cause mass destruction upon our home planet. Someone like you, with your powers, could assist in our quest to banish these creatures forever…'

'I'm up for it…' Crippler said.

'But first…' she said, and passed a hand across Crippler's scarred face, '…this will get us off to a great start. You are a beautiful human again…what is your name, great one?'

He felt the change happen and his face alter noticeably for the better, as the strange magic took effect and corrected his features.

'Death Cop…' he said.

A black cloak suddenly descended over Crippler and he felt himself elevate off the ground, and rise upwards into the grey and gloomy post-Apocalyptic skies above the empty deserted wastes of West Cumbria. Anywhere was better than here…

He heard the woman say, 'I'm taking to the Red Planet…not Mars, as you might think…no, this is another Red Planet…much farther away…'

Before Crippler knew it he was standing in a clinically white circular domed-room, traversing space at unbelievable velocity, burning through the star-system. Huge windows decked the room, giving a panoramic full-view of space and its vast awesome plains. A vicinity Crippler had only since dreamt of exploring.

'Your enemy Keaton is our enemy…we need you infiltrate the criminal classes of our world, find Keaton and his cohorts, and exterminate them. In return, you will gain citizenship to our world…a world which we must protect, and with your assistance will.'

Death Cop didn't waste time considering.

'It would be my pleasure,' he said, 'Earth is done and dusted.'

'Thank you, sir,' said the woman, 'And you will be made most welcome…Death Cop.'

Crippler smiled sardonically.

'Call me Beau…Beau Crippler. I only go by the name Death Cop on my days off.'

THE END.

IT
GREGORY KH BRYANT

HOW I got into this place, I don't remember.

It is all lost in the endlessly unfolding amnesia of an interminable nightmare. Long endless halls of unfinished wood, floors, walls and ceiling all—the vicious splinters have torn the soles from my feet. I leave trails of bloody footprints upon the biting wooden floors. My fingers and hands, my arms and legs are lacerated with splinters. I bleed.

Naked flames burning from the gas lamps on the walls illumine this filthy place with a sickly yellow light. Ancient black grease is caked in the corners.

I've been lost here forever.

Piles of rotting and half-digested viscera lie in sloppy heaps upon the painful floors. They look as if they should have been the entrails of a bird or a rat murdered by a feral cat and only partially devoured, vomited forth again, and left to lie in the yellow light like lurid obscenities.

But no sparrow or rat gave rise to these heaps of rotting intestine, of stinking offal. The mounds are everywhere, and they are huge. They cast long shadows upon the splintering floors, and I cower often within those inky shadows. I tremble to think what things they could have been, that should give rise to such massive heaps of putrid entrails.

The close air is thick with the stench of decomposition.

This thing—it is hunting me.

This thing that has slaughtered all these creatures. It hunts me. Through these ceaseless, labyrinthine, these painful halls, where every step lacerates my feet with splinters, this thing hunts me.

What this repulsive thing is, I don't know. I have heard its distant shrieks howling through the halls. My blood congeals with hopeless, helpless terror.

It is bestial and remorseless.

Ultimately, it will find me.

I can do nothing but postpone the inevitable moment of my own disembowelment.

Pain. All is pain.

I have never seen this thing, though I know it by the half-digested corpses it has strewn like breadcrumbs in its wake.

It knows me. It will find me.

I loved her there.

Who she is and how she came to me is also lost in infinite forgetfulness. I explored her with my hands and she responded to my touch, like a timid corpse experiencing its first tremors of rigor mortis.

But my coward fear drives me on, through ceaseless hall of naked wood that tear my flesh with every step. She follows, pale, tremulous and fearful. Her lips are blue. Her eyes, flat and dead. No lustre of life escapes them.

We have never spoken. Never once has a sound passed between us.

We found ourselves in a suffocating cell. The sallow glow of the naked lamps extruding from the walls cast paranoiac shadows long into the narrow hall beyond. My body pierced with countless splinters, and she trusted me, blindly, to protect her.

We crawled under a narrow wooden bench—a box, that looked very much like a cheap coffin, the kind in which the corpses of the nameless poor are often buried.

And the monstrous thing that pursued us came itself into the narrow cell wherein we hid.

She and I clung trembling, each to the other, like incestuous children hiding from a brutal and drunken father.

It has come. It knows we are here. And it knows where we hide.

But it has no interest in us for the moment.

It has found other amusements.

The inhuman screams of some creature, some pitiable half-human thing, its dying shrieks tear our ears as it is flayed alive and eviscerated, only but inches from us.

We are separated from this hellish murder by a narrow purple shadow and a thin panel of wood. Rivulets of blood seep under the panel, pooling under our naked bodies.

The obscene sucking and belching of this thing as it greedily devours the living flesh of this sorry creature shakes the unsteady bench.

And then, once done with its feast, a long and tortured silence followed at last by the vomiting. The tiny cell is filled with the sickening sounds of this thing's retching.

We can see the shadow of it cast upon the wall behind our tentative bench. The shadow shudders, it convulses, and a stinking ejaculation of bloated and still living viscera spews out from its monstrous mouth, upon the floor. Foul blood splatters the walls and the ceiling.

This thing, this monster, whatever it is, is satisfied for now.

It knows me. Us. This nameless she, and I. It will find us, in time.

There is no hurry.

THE END

DEATH COMES IN KALEIDOSCOPE
BENJAMIN WELTON

THE TIREDNESS in Jack had reached the point where everything felt fuzzy. The steering wheel, the creases in his pants, and the seat he was sitting on—all fuzzy. In Jack's mind, everything had a soft edge to it, and when he was tired, he imagined the edges as brightly coloured and floating outlines that made the type of noises one would hear in a 1950s sci-fi film. When things reached this point, Jack had to sleep. Hell, Jack needed to sleep. But he couldn't. Not on this night and not on this job. Worse still, Jack needed to be awake and alert in order to hate with every inch of his body the man blathering next to him.

"This would be a lot better if they reduced the music a little, know what I mean? C'mon, that Ted the Tarantula guy is great. Remember that one about the guy who was set up with tickets to a baseball game and named his mistress as his second? I mean, with his actual wife on the call and everything. Ha-ha, classic."

Paulie had been assigned to Jack and he was as pleasant as syphilis. To be fair, there wasn't a mean bone in Paulie's body, but he was annoying as all hell. Ever since starting the job in Boston, Paulie had talked non-stop about the weather, the road, and the days of the week (Paulie was the only man in history who preferred Tuesday). However, what really got Paulie's tongue rolling was the radio. Paulie loved FM radio, especially the various local zoos. He would repeat bits back to Jack as if he hadn't just heard the same thing in Worcester or Waterbury, and most egregious of all, Paulie would go up and down about how he could do a better job on the air. For almost ten hours, Jack suffered through one hack idea after another. By the time they reached Scranton, Jack had decided on killing Paulie with the crowbar in the glove compartment.

Normally, Jack was an even-tempered guy, but something about the job just didn't sit right with him. Paulie's vacuous babble didn't help, but if Jack was being really honest, he'd have to say that his anger and irritation had to do with the job and not Paulie's lame ideas.

JACK AND Paulie met each other outside of a nondescript building in Cambridge. Jack had been tipped off about the job by Rocco, the bartender at Vinny's. Rocco knew that Jack was in the middle of an expensive divorce, so he decided to throw the Pollock a favour. Paulie, on the other hand, was being set up. Paulie was a low level pusher and a sometime bookie who was primarily a stumblebum who could barely hold a job as an off-the-books cook in a Mexican restaurant. Again, nobody could hate Paulie because he was such a nice, clueless oaf, but everyone agreed that it would be better if he weren't around. Idiocy isn't cheap, after all. So, accordingly, Paulie's boss at the Mexican restaurant, who doubled as a bagman for some boys in Providence, put Paulie in line with what he called a "sugary sweet deal" that he knew would go sour. And when it did go sour, Paulie would get the big one and everything would be free and easy afterwards.

So there Jack and Paulie stood on the morning when they unwittingly signed up for their own deaths. After saying hi and after Paulie started rifling off jokes so terrible that they made Jack's teeth hurt, they were ushered inside by a gigantic and unibrowed man in black leather. As it turned out, this was Chabworz, the muscle for Hooza Yamadayev, alias The Bird. The Bird was the head of a group of Chechens who were known for cutting off fingers and the occasional head. Ostensibly, The Bird was into drugs, guns, and the occasional bank robbery, but it was whispered that The Bird sent most of his money overseas in order to fund bearded guys who wore black and shouted "Allahu Akbar" whenever they felt the need to blow themselves up in front of women, children, and military convoys. Now, by his own admission, he had something he just couldn't sell.

"We tried everything. Black market in Turkey, internet, even mail order. No one will take it because they all say it's a fake. So, if we can't sell it, then we're going to burn it. Now all we need is a driver who will take it to where we say and burn it," The Bird said.

"One man job?" Jack asked.

"Doesn't matter. Could be or could be two. You're both here even though I only expected you, Jack. But if we can split your money, we will. Why don't you take him, Jack?" The Bird's smile was so broad and shit-eating that it made Jack nauseous.

"With all due respect, this job isn't too tough. One person could do it and do it right."

"That is unless we ask that person to go somewhere dangerous or difficult," The Bird finally took a bite out of the sandwich that had been by his elbow the whole time.

"If you're asking for something north across the border, I can still do it alone."

"No, I think I like the idea of two men better. More secure, plus I'll bother God less with my prayers because I know you'll protect each other. But in truth it's not a bad job. Just take the car we give you, drive it here (The Bird pointed to what looked like the middle of West Virginia on his desk's globe), and burn everything. Ok?"

Jack turned to Paulie and saw a useless imbecile. For his part, Paulie winked at Jack and then started talking to The Bird about some statistic he'd heard earlier that day on the radio. Apparently, men who were castrated lived longer on average. The Bird cocked an eyebrow, Jack looked at the ground and winced, while Chabworz farted in the corner. Only Paulie laughed and asked "Isn't that something, guys?"

JACK AND Paulie crossed over from Pennsylvania into West Virginia at 1 a.m. Jack had gotten so tired that he decided to call an audible—instead of driving deeper into the state like The Bird wanted, he decided to find an isolated spot nearby and do the job. They'd set the car alight, find their way to the nearest motel, then call a cab or catch a bus to the nearest airport, which, according to the GPS, was in Morgantown. Jack was comfortable with the decision; Paulie was too far gone with a late night poll on WVAQ to care about anything else.

"You know, maybe we should do a radio show after this. I mean, I used to do some radio back when I was still in 'college.'" For added emphasis, Paulie put his hands up and made air quotes. Apparently, he expected Jack to care.

"I was too busy listening to the radio all night to ever go to class. Besides, my school didn't teach broadcasting, so I didn't care. Just did it to please the old man. You know what I mean?" For some reason, Paulie rolled the window down, even though it was no warmer than 40 outside.

"For Christ's sake, Paulie. Put that window up."

"I like the fresh air, man. It reminds me of New Hampshire," Paulie dramatically sniffed the air, then made a Mr. Yuck face to no laughs.

"Will you just put it up, please!"

Jack was having trouble concentrating. The multi-coloured haze that he had been chalking up to exhaustion now hurt. Everything hurt, and it all emanated from his forehead. Simply put, Jack had a headache that was seconds away from becoming a migraine.

Jack had his first migraine when he was ten. It had come two days after his parents had checked him out of the hospital. The week before, Jack had barely survived a fall from his father's ladder while fooling around with some of the neighbourhood kids. The doctors kept him around in order to make sure his young brain wasn't too damaged, although Jack always assumed that he had royally screwed something up there, for the migraines never stopped. They came frequently, and on a good month Jack only got two as opposed to his usual four. The fact that he got hit by a car when he was in high school and thus sustained more head trauma did not help matters whatsoever. The migraines made it hard for Jack to hold down a job, and the constant poverty made it even harder to hold a good woman like Mary Alice.

Now, with the nitwit Paulie by his side, Jack's head was making it hard to just hold the steering wheel. Worse still, somewhere near Mount Morris, Jack realized that his nose was bleeding a little. Definitely not good.

"Ha-ha, it's killing me. Listen to this guy, he's good, but I could do better. Check it out, if I ran this show, I'd cut some of the music, especially since no one wants music this early in the morning. What I'd do is this: I'd have a theme for the day, like "Meat of the Day" or something. Then I'd take some calls, and maybe then I'd play something like "War of the Sexes." You know what that is? That's where you get one guy and one girl, who then try and answer questions about the other sex. It's a classic, but if I ran it, I'd incorporate the theme of the day into it. For instance, I'd do "War of the Sexes" involving questions about meat. Hey, what about it?"

Paulie stared at Jack for an uncomfortably long time. Jack, wide-eyed, couldn't wrap his head around the idiocy of what he'd just heard. Jack's head felt like it was about to burst. He had to stop the car in order to press his hands against his temples or just do anything to combat the pain. On the radio, the opening strains of The Bee Gees's "Massachusetts" started playing.

Then, without warning, the car shook. It was soft at first and felt like the vibrations of a passing semi. But, according to a road sign, Jack and Paulie were in some place called Cheat Lake and there were no semis around. Jack tried to ignore the feeling at first. He was too concerned with keeping the vomit in his mouth and the blood in his nose to worry about some rattle. For his part, Paulie got out of the car and walked towards the trunk in order to see what was causing the vibrations.

"Hey, Jack. Did The Bird ever tell you what it is that we're hauling?"

"No, why?" Jack barely got the words out because he was spitting and yawning so much.

"Well, what about the tools. Like, is the kerosene in the trunk?"

"What's the problem, Paulie? What are you worried about?"

"It's just that there seems to be something alive back here."

Paulie's answer jolted Jack awake a little bit. Something alive—that couldn't be good. It suddenly occurred to Jack that The Bird had sent him and Paulie on a murder mission without their knowledge. He worried that there was some man or woman bound with rope and tape in the trunk, and the only reason that they were kicking now was due to some sedative wearing off. Jack got even more sick thinking about burning somebody alive.

After wiping his mouth and slapping himself a little, Jack joined Paulie at the back of the car.

"What do you think is in there?" Paulie had his hands on the trunk's hood in order to feel it vibrate.

"Only way to know is to open it."

"Hey, man. That's all you."

"C'mon, Paulie. I've had to listen to you babble all night, so you owe me one. Actually, you owe me more than that, but we'll be square if you help me see this thing through, ok?"

Paulie threw his hands in the air, then used them to oddly massage his bald head.

"Okay, okay. We'll do it, but if it's some kind of monster, then I'm running back to New England."

"Whatever, just grab the kerosene when you see it. Alright, 1-2-3..."

SIX WEEKS before, Chabworz had gone back to the old country because his brother was having a problem. Chabworz hated his brother, but since he overlooked The Bird's overland supply routes into Turkey, Chabworz had to make sure he was healthy, happy, and doing the job right. Unfortunately, he and the entire village were too scared to do anything, let alone leave their homes and mule guns and drugs through at least one warzone. The reason: Chabworz's brother swore that there was a monster in the mountains.

According to him and the local imam, some kind of creature was responsible for killing at least three girls in the last two weeks. The one girl who had survived claimed that it looked like an extraordinarily large wolf, but its colour was all wrong. It looked like some kind of green-yellow mixture, and even though her vision was halfway clouded with her own blood, her eyes convinced her that the thing was decidedly unnatural.

"A demon from hell" is what she called it.

Chabworz, who was known as "Fearless" in the village, chalked up all the stories to the abandoned tower that overlooked the village. Ever since he was a little boy, everyone called the tower haunted. Stories percolated that the tower had once been part of an ancient fort. Some elders claimed that the fort and the former village it once protected had been founded by Christians who had all been killed during the Caucasian War of the 19th century. Others, some of whom claimed to have seen the site with their own eyes, argued that there was nothing Christian about the site whatsoever. To them, the ruined tower was a demonic site dedicated to devil worship. They simply called it "Satan's Tower."

This contingent warned Chabworz not to go after the creature. It had to be a demon after all, and Chabworz, whom everyone knew cared little for Allah, could not defeat the monster alone. Casting aside their warnings as superstitious prattle, Chabworz set off towards the ruined tower with the Dragunov that he had carried during the first war against the Russians.

By the time Chabworz reached the ruins, it had started to snow. The thick sea of white made everything pretty except for the ugly tower, which was made of black-grey stone. Upon closer inspection, Chabworz could make out little pictograms everywhere on the crumbling walls, and on the other side of a balistraria, Chabworz found some graffiti written in a language he did not know. For some reason, this made Chabworz uneasy, but he suppressed this strange feeling in order to set up a small camp for the night. He unrolled his sleeping bag and put a small pillow underneath his right elbow. Chabworz then attached the night vision scope and got into the prone firing position. After testing the scope by doing a few short sweeps of the area, Chabworz began to wait.

The hours went by slowly. Chabworz rarely moved from his position, and after a few quick scans that had been caused by strange noises, Chabworz mostly kept his rifle pointed south towards the village. Near midnight, a bored Chabworz checked his magazine. He put his index finger on the top bullet and pretended to press hard on the casing. Then Chabworz did something rare: he smiled.

Right before Chabworz loaded the magazine for a second time, he saw a black shape move in the periphery. Chabworz turned his head to the left and the right, but could not relocate the shape. Chabworz was in the process of rationalizing what he'd seen, when his head started to hurt. Chabworz, who never got headaches, began convulsing on the ground. He screamed in the hopes of dulling the imaginary knives that were impaling his brain. He even vomited.

After wiping his mouth, Chabworz began seeing strange colours everywhere. The rocks, the snow, and the stones of the ruined fort began to dance with green, red, orange, and yellow outlines. Chabworz blinked a million times, but he could not get rid of the Technicolor nightmare around him. Worse still, in the midst of all the colours, Chabworz could hear heavy footsteps approaching. It was not an animal—Chabworz knew that for sure. Then again, they sounded too large to be human. Plus, no human could make the awful stench that almost knocked Chabworz unconscious. Chabworz would later tell The Bird that it smelled like sewage mixed with sulphur. In the retelling, Chabworz and The Bird both gagged a little.

As the terrible smell grew stronger and the colours began to eclipse everything, Chabworz started to panic. He still had his body in the firing position and out of fear he had moved his finger from the receiver to the trigger. Chabworz could hear the voice of his father admonishing him for such an unsafe act, but Chabworz not only kept his finger on the trigger, but he even depressed it slightly. Right before Chabworz pulled, a new voice entered his head. It was speaking in an unknown language and sounded muffled. It was obviously chanting, and if Chabworz hadn't fired, the voice would've kept on chanting until Chabworz was deaf. But somehow everything—the colours, the headache, the strange voice—ended as soon as Chabworz fired the shot.

Dazed, Chabworz began stumbling among the ruins with the rifle in his hands. He banged his knee several times, and at one point he broke the rifle's scope after falling into a depression that had once been a room in the tower. He vomited for a second time, but he retained enough of his senses to take a look at what had just come violently out of his stomach. It was mostly bile, but Chabworz could discern something very black in it. Upon bending down to get an even closer look, Chabworz noticed that there were tracks leading away from his vomit. They were deep, three-toed tracks that led off into the distance. Chabworz placed his right hand in one of them and could feel the mud underneath the snow. He placed his left hand in the next track, then repeated this process until he found the thing motionless on its side. It was close to the top of the mountain and right beside a piece of an ancient wall. Near what could've been its ribs was a bullet hole that was not bleeding. As Chabworz placed his fingers into the wound, he realized that the creature was still breathing. They were shallow, barely alive intakes of air, but the ungodly creature still lived. And when Chabworz gently rolled it over onto its back, he became the first human being in over a thousand years to see its face.

THE TRUNK did not immediately open. Whatever was inside had been so tightly squeezed into the trunk that it now blocked the hood. Jack went back into the passenger seat and opened the glove compartment. He pulled out the crowbar and slid it under the taillights. After several strong lifts that caused Jack to grunt and groan like he was copulating, the trunk finally opened.

Immediately, the colours that Jack had been seeing the entire drive kicked up again, but this time they were so strong that they obscured everything around him. The formerly dark blue lake was now purple. Even Paulie's white, bald head had turned a neon green. As for the migraine, Jack was no longer experiencing it. Instead of a strong headache, Jack was now hosting a marching band in his head. The small dribble of blood was now gushing from his nose. Within seconds, Jack began losing consciousness from the loss of blood and water. Right before going out, Jack saw a multi-coloured arm shoot out from the trunk and rip Paulie's throat out. Instead of red, Paulie bleed hot pink.

"Massachusetts?"

The deputy turned to his partner who stood next to the two corpses.

"Looks like these guys were far from home. Wonder what they were up to."

"From what I can see, they had something in the trunk that wasn't in there of their own free will. If I had to guess, I'd say they were gangsters trying to kill off a hostage. The hostage, being pretty mad about having to ride from Massachusetts to Cheat Lake in the trunk, jumped this guy first and went to work with a lot of fury. Just look at that throat!"

"This might sound crazy, but that looks more like an animal's work than any human. But, why in the world would they drive so far with an animal in the trunk?"

"Don't know, Dell. This looks like one hell of a mystery. I guess we ought to start pounding on doors and see what people know."

"That's just the thing. There aren't any houses around here. Just the lake and the road."

"Wait a minute. Isn't there something down that way?" The deputy pointed to a tree-lined road that curved to the north.

"Nope. Back in the day there used to be some kind of resort out that way, but it hasn't seen any occupants since the Depression. We could check it out, but it's just ruins."

The deputies looked at each other for a brief moment. Then, without saying a word, they both decided that the abandoned resort wasn't worth it.

"Alright, let's get the white coats out here so they can bag these two up. And for God's sake, turn that radio off. I can't stand that crap."

THE END.

JUST THE RIGHT ADDITION
RICK MCQUISTON

'JUST THE right addition,' Lenny recalled Ansel saying. 'That's what I need, the right addition.'

Lenny knew the guy was strange, but he didn't know he was dangerous.

Now he was finding out the hard way just how dangerous his neighbour really was. Now he was learning what trust, or at the very least, indifference to a person's eccentricities, could turn into.

Dust drifted down from the top of the hastily-constructed pine box and into Lenny's face. He squeezed his eyes shut and tried to turn his head to the side, but since his eyelids were the only part of his body he could still move, he simply had to endure the discomfort.

In his rapidly-deteriorating psyche, Lenny wished Ansel had done a better job building the box. He remembered his would-be murdering neighbour muttering something about having to be quick, that the drugs in his addition would wear off soon and then he'd have to take him out the messy way. That was why the box in which Lenny now found himself in and was so rickety; Ansel had put it together quickly.

Time lost all meaning for Lenny. Seconds dripped into minutes, which in turn slid into hours. He couldn't tell the difference. He had no feeling in his body (not even his stomach) so he couldn't tell if he was hungry.

He could starve to death and he wouldn't even know it.

What had Ansel meant by the right addition? Right addition to what?

Lenny hoped he would die before he found out.

And then he heard a voice.

At first, he thought it was in his head, but then realized it was from above.

It was Ansel, and he was talking to someone.

Lenny held his breath and listened as hard as he could.

'Easy now,' Ansel said in an affectionate tone. 'Just settle down. Be patient. You have to wait for the fertilizer to work.'

Fertilizer? Fertilizer for what?

The questions swirled around Lenny's deteriorating mind like soap down a drain. He tried to find an answer to each one but couldn't.

Who's he talking to? Is he going kill me?

'Lenny? I know you can still hear me. I must apologize for the effects of the drugs I gave you, they are my own concoction. Bernizene thryocit with a dash of Cynthothymine. 400 milligrams did the trick. I suppose I fancy myself something of an amateur chemist, so please bear with me.'

Lenny heard movement around him. He could sense something seeping into the box.

'Look at the bright side, Lenny: you won't feel a thing. After all, now you're just fertilizer.'

Thin black roots sneaked in through the cracks in the box. Wood splintered to allow them access to the interior. They groped for purchase, quickly latching onto Lenny's body.

'You see, Lenny, she grows best with live food, live fertilizer. That's why I put you in the box, to keep you alive. You would've died if I simply buried you.'

More noises. More tendrils exploring, feeling, reaching.

'Yes, yes, my pet, he's a good one. His body is just right.'

Lenny heard something hiss and growl.

'Just right, just the right addition to my garden.'

The pine box then gave way to the mass of roots pressing in on it, and Lenny tried to scream, but couldn't because he was still paralyzed.

THE END.

TERROR ON SNAIL ISLAND
GREGORY KH BRYANT

Intrepid reporter Katie Hyland has come to Oakie Island to interview Dr. Weller, the world renowned geneticist. He is attempting to solve world hunger by developing a method to increase the size of animals. Things go awry when the process begins to affect the snails for which the place is famous. They begin a rampage, and Katie attempts to escape.

Now read on…

Part Eleven

Dr. Weller: The… the thing… the snail…

Camera cuts to show us what Dr. Weller sees. Slowly the monstrous snail emerges from its shell. Eyes on stalks and its foot appear from the lower edge. The eye stalks look about.

They see Dr. Weller and Wright pinned to the floor.

Camera cuts to show us the two helpless scientists from the giant snail's point of view, looking down upon them, with a weirdly shifting double-vision effect to suggest what the snail might see with its independently moving eyes.

Seeing them, the snail begins to move toward them, pushing over the tables that have futilely fenced it into the corner. It moves slowly, inexorably.

Dr. Weller begins to flail his forearms in a useless attempt to free himself from the snail's slime. He begins to pant with terror.

Dr. Weller: No… no…

Wright: What is happening? What?

Dr. Weller: The snail. It's crawling over the tables… It's… coming for us…

Wright: It's… what? Oh, no… it's… no...

The snail moves purposely, relentlessly. Wright and Weller grow more frantic as the monster draws nearer. They scream for Burke.

Dr. Weller and Wright: Burke! Burke! Come here now! Now! BUUU-U-RKE!!

A quick cut of the camera shows us Burke in the cabin. He is sitting in a chair, his feet up on a wooden foot rest, reading a magazine, and sipping from a hip flask. All is silent in the cabin.

The echo of a barely heard sound impinges upon the ear. What was that? Burke is suddenly alert. He looks up from his magazine, cups an ear.

Burke: Huh? Wuzzat?

He stands up from the chair, holsters his hip flask, and listens, alert, facing the door. Will he stay, or will he go to see what that distant commotion could be?

Back to the laboratory.

The snail has reached the two scientists.
It is tentatively testing them by touching their shoes with its lower tentacles.
Camera zooms in on the snail's face. Extreme close-up on its mouth. It is salivating.
It takes a cautious bite of a shoe. And then another. The snail begins eating the two scientists as nonchalantly as it would a leaf.
Dr. Weller and Wright go insane with terror. They scream madly.

Dr. Weller: AAAAAAAAAAAAAAAAAAAAAAHHHHHH!!!!!

Wright: AAAAAAAAUUUUUUUUUGGGGGHHHHHH!

Giant Snail: Nom, nom, nom.

Fade to Black

Cut to jungle.

Night has fallen. Captain Philips, Katie and Lisa are still finding their way through the thick growth. Their clothes are torn, in ribbons. They are exhausted, faces grimed, eyes haunted.

Philips leads the way, aided only by a small penlight. Its

tiny beam cuts a thin and hesitant line through the dark silhouettes of leaves and vines.

The three move cautiously through the thick undergrowth. Captain Philips carefully examines each foot of jungle before them before taking a wary step. Katie and Lisa, close behind him, carefully place their feet in the spot Captain Philips has stepped in.

And in this exhausting manner, they make their painstaking way.

Philips pauses, and with a small jack-knife he cuts a gouge into the bow of a tree, blazing their trail.

Katie leans against Philips as he takes the moment to mark the tree.

Katie (Exhausted): I can't believe this island is so big. It's been hours.

Captain Philips: We're lost, Katie. I don't know if we've been wandering in circles. I doubt it. But honestly, I don't know. But I do know we are lost.

Katie: But the harbour. It was so close. It was just a five minute drive…

Captain Philips: Which you and I only drove down once, and Lisa here…

Lisa: Not too many times. I mostly stayed at the compound. It was Rick and Terry… who met the ferry at the harbour… (She chokes at the memory of her two dead friends).

Captain Philips (finishing the thought for Lisa): …every two weeks. And they're gone now. Not that they'd have been much help, anyway. The utility road is gone. It's been completely overgrown since just yesterday.

Katie: Oh, Dwight… what will we do?

Captain Philips: One thing's for sure. We have to stay alive. And somehow, we have to get back to the mainland to warn the officials. If Weller's reagent were to spread… or if any of these things on this island were to escape, and to continue their wild growth… their insane reproduction…

Katie: Oh! Dwight… what a nightmare!

Captain Philips: At least we've got far enough away from the compound that those confounded snails aren't haunting our every step.

He takes a quick glance upward. The camera follows his glance and we see that the branches and leaves overhead are mercifully free of the monstrous snails. For the moment.

Captain Philips: Somehow, we've got to find high ground, if we can't find the shore. From there, we'll be able to take our bearings, at least. Perhaps set up a signal fire that might be seen at sea.

Katie (Looking helplessly about. The jungle is thick and hard upon them. Heavy growth brushes up against them at every turn. They cannot see much further than the tips of their fingers held out at arm's length): But which way?

Captain Philips (Shaking his head ruefully): I honestly don't know, Katie. I'm a man of the sea. Out there, on the sea, I can survive. But this jungle is something completely outside my knowledge. Here, I am truly a babe in the woods.

They trudge on.

And then, a light rainfall begins. Their tattered clothes are slickened with moisture.

Lisa: Oh... oh... I don't think I can bear much more of this!

At that moment, the beam of Philip's penlight bounces off a shining surface several years ahead.

Katie: What is that?

Captain Philips: I don't know. It seems...

We can barely make it out in the darkness, and through the confusion of leaves and heavy growth. It seems a shining concavity of a sort, with white walls. The three make their way closer to it.

Katie: Why, it looks like a cave!

Captain Philips: It is. Or it surely seems to be.

They stand at the opening, peering into the strange darkness. The cave mouth is nearly twelve feet tall. Captain Philips lays his hand upon the wall of the cave. It is smooth.

Captain Philips: I don't get it. This feels almost like linoleum. Or plastic. Or porcelain. (He turns to Lisa) Lisa, is this one of Dr. Weller's doings? Did he build a secret laboratory, out here in the jungle?

Lisa: I don't know. I never heard him talk of anything like this. It's... strange...

Captain Philips (Shining the beam of his penlight into the depths, and peering in): Yes, it is strange. It looks like a hallway... that turns off to the right... down there... Well, maybe it can give us a little shelter, a place to wait out this rain.

Katie (Peering skyward): I hope it doesn't last.

Captain Philips (Studying the sky with the eye of a professional): No. This should be just a slight shower. It'll be over in a moment. But we may as well take advantage of what shelter we can find. Let's go.

He strides into the cave with the porcelain walls. Katie and Lisa follow close behind.

Captain Philips (Playing the light of the penlight into the depths of the curving cavern): I'm curious. I want to see where this goes.

Katie: Are you sure?

Captain Philips: If there's anything lurking in here, I want to face it head on.

Katie: Okay... lead on.

The three of them move cautiously into the cavern.

Captain Philips: Odd. It just keeps turning off to the right.

Katie: And getting smaller.

Captain Philips (Growing dubious): ...yes.

Lisa: And the walls are all curved.

Katie: …and the ceiling.

Captain Philips: No corners…

Lisa: … almost like…

Captain Philips: It's… do you smell that?

Katie: It… smells like something's died.

Captain Philips: Yes. The stench gets worse, the further in we go.

Katie: Yes. It's…

Lisa points to a blackened and shapeless mass of dead flesh lying in a congealed pile before them.

Lisa: What's… what's that horrible thing?

Dawning understanding comes to all three of them, simultaneously.

Katie: Oh, no… it's… it's…

Lisa: We're inside a…

Captain Philips (Abruptly): Let's get out of here!

They turn and flee.

Stumbling outside, they run away from it, climbing a steep hillside. They come to a stop near the top of it, and all tumble into heap. They are all panting heavily.

The rain has stopped. Skittish clouds scutter before a

cold and starry sky.

They look back, and Captain Philips directs the beam from his penlight to the thing below them. From here, we can see that what they have found is the shell of a monstrous snail. It is forty feet across, and over fourteen feet deep.

For a moment, Captain Philips, Katie and Lisa stare at it in dumb silence, too stunned to speak.
Finally, Captain Philips finds his voice.

Captain Philips: Look at that thing… it's a monster… it's…

Lisa (Puzzled): But it's dead. Why did it die?

Captain Philips: It… I don't know. Perhaps it crushed itself under its own weight. Perhaps… I… don't know.

Katie cowers against Captain Philips, leaning her head against his chest.

Katie: Oh, Dwight. It… it… what has Doctor Weller done? What has he unleashed upon the world?

Captain Philips shakes his head slowly.

Captain Philips: Who can say? This thing… this monstrous thing that he has created with his reagent… it must be stopped somehow.

Lisa: But… but how?

Captain Philips, suddenly alert, holds up his hand.

Captain Philips: Just a moment! Wait!

Katie: What is it, Dwight?

Captain Philips snaps his penlight off. Darkness envelopes the trio.

Captain Philips: Give it a moment. Let our eyes adjust to the darkness… yes. Yes, I am right!

Lisa: What? What is it?

Captain Philips: The shore! Just down there! Between the boles of those trees below us. You can just see the starlight reflected from the surface.

Katie and Lisa peer into the darkness below.

Lisa: … I don't…

Katie: Yes! You're right! It's the sea! At last! A way away from this terrible, terrible island.

Lisa: But how? Can we build a raft? Just us?

Captain Philips (A long pause as he considers Lisa's point): … she's right. We have no tools. Those are back at the harbour. Maybe we could follow the shore around till we got back to it, whichever direction it is. But there's no guarantee that the harbour is a safe place any more. In fact, it's a sure bet that things are worse there now than ever before…

All three fall to silence. Finally Lisa breaks the silence.

Lisa: What about the shell?

Captain Philips: The shell?

Lisa: Snail shells float in water. They have compartments. They... they float. Can't we, maybe, scooch it down to the water, and maybe use it like a raft?

Captain Philips (Thoughtfully): It sounds pretty desperate...

Katie: But so are we... desperate, that is.

Captain Philips (Granting her a grudging smile): So we are. I wonder, though, if we have enough strength between the three of us to move it?

Lisa: Snail shells are not particularly heavy. Their strength is in their structure, the way they're built.

Katie: Maybe we can push it, and get it to glide down on top of the undergrowth?

Captain Philips: Well, let's give it a try.

They make their way back down the slope, and to the monstrous snail shell. As they stand in its shadow, under the stars, it towers over them.

Captain Philips: Well, let's put our shoulders to it!

The three of them lean against it with their shoulders.

Captain Philips: On three, let's push. One... two... three...

All three of them push, and manage to get the shell to rock slightly upward.

Captain Philips: That's good. That's very promising.

Let's try it again, but this time, let's see if we can get it to rocking.

Katie and Lisa: Okay!

They lean against the huge shell a second time, and on Captain Philips' command, they begin pushing it with a 'heave-ho!' motion. It rocks forward, then back. Then forward again. With each push, the shell rocks a bit higher, and shifts an inch or two further.

Captain Philips (Chanting): Heave… ho! Heave… ho! Heave…

Inch by inch they edge the huge snail shell down an incline. It rocks in an ever-increasing arc.

At last, success.

The shell slides down a steepening slope, upon the rain-slickened grasses. It slips with increasing speed, between the boles of the trees. At last, it tumbles off a short cliff, into the sea.

Captain Philips, Katie and Lisa, plainly exhausted, give a weak cheer, and hurry down the slope to catch up with the bobbing snail shell.

They manage to catch up with it in time, before it drifts away with the currents. Lisa leaps down gingerly upon the shell, which causes it to buoy slightly away from the short bluff. Captain Philips assists Katie, holding her hand and partly dangling her as she finds her footing upon it.

With Katie now upon the shell, Captain Philips prepares to leap.

Katie: Be careful, Dwight! It's very slick!

Captain Philips gives his head a nod to show he understands, and then leaps from the island. He bounds upon the slippery surface of the shell, which drops deeply into the water as he lands. He almost loses his footing, and nearly slides into the sea.

Katie grabs his hand, and Lisa holds onto Katie. Between them all, they manage to get Captain Philips securely upon the shell.

Captain Philips (Looking back at the island still near at hand): I wish we had poles to push away with.

Katie: I think the current is taking us away. Slowly, but it seems we are drifting past the island, and maybe, eventually, away from it.

Captain Philips takes everything in—sea, wavelets, the island, and the sky above—with the critical eye of a sailor.

Captain Philips: I believe you're right, Katie.

Fade to black.

Cut to Scene.

The cabin door opens. Burke steps outside. He looks around.
The grass is wild, growing almost as tall as he, except for those places where he laid down the lye. The wheelbarrow is near the porch, still with bags of lye upon it.
Burke looks about, through the darkness of the jungle night.
Sounds off to his left, in the darkness, catch his

attention. He looks that way.

The camera shows us what he sees.

The laboratory is ruined. The roof, collapsed, the walls, blasted away. In the wreckage stands the huge snail that has just finished devouring Doctor Weller and Wright. It has grown beyond all sane proportions, towering monstrously over the ruins of the laboratory.

Burke, standing on the wooden balcony of the cabin, only a few dozen feet away, stares up at the towering snail.

The snail's eyes, on its huge stalks, turn and stare back at Burke.

Burke: Now, just look at you. (He shakes his head with the philosophic unconcern of an ancient man.) You have really got yourself all out of hand. Got no business being so squanderously huge. Not you. Not no garden variety snail, not nohow, no way.

The snail turns its eyes to look fully upon Burke. We see him from the snail's view, the superimposed double-images we saw before. Burke is looking up at the snail, his head disproportionally large to the rest of his body.

Camera cuts back to show us Burke on the balcony, as if we were standing next to him. He is still shaking his head, tut-tutting the monster before him as the thing begins to creep toward him.

Burke: Yeah... I kind of expected somethin' like this was gonna go on down. That Weller feller... seemed smart enough, if you didn't press him too close, but... well, y'know, he just dint seem to have too much common sense about him. Nope. Smart as he was, or he thunk he was, he just dint seem to have the sense that God gave to your average head o' cabbage. Well, that's all just too bad. Just, too, too bad. Seems like all these experts dint know half of what all they was going on about, after all. Idn't that right? (He casts a sharp eye up toward the snail, as it slowly draws near.)

Burke: Looks Like I'm gonna to have to be doin' somethin'. Can't be lettin' you go wildin' all about, can I? (He observes that the monstrous snail is approaching. He nods his head, as if holding a conversation with it.) Yeah... that's right, old fellow... come along with me. Seems you're not too comfortable, neither, eh? Yeah. You never wanted to grow so big, I don't think. You look like you got a hurtin' on you. Well, I got some stuff down this way to take care of your problems. Mine, too, and ever' one else's, I'm s'posin'. Well, follow me, friend. We're gonna be all right, you and me. We'll be fine, and all your friends, too.

Burke wades through the thick grass, stepping carefully, and moving past the huge head of the monstrous snail. He makes his way to the Quonset hut, and there, to the two large tanks holding the compound's supply of gasoline. The tanks tower over Burke, standing twelve feet high, and sixteen or so feet long.
The monstrous snail follows slowly but ominously behind Burke, catching up to him at the tanks. It peers over the tanks and looks down at Burke.

Burke (Nodding his head in approval): Yeah, there ye' go. That's the thing. Good boy.

He looks up as the snail as it peers down at him, as it begins to climb over the tank. Burke smiles. He opens the spigot to the tank. Gasoline pours out into the ground. It cascades through the thick grass, inundating the countless thousands of snails that crawl throughout it.

Burke (Smiling): Who's a good snail, huh? Are we a good snail?

The eye stalks of the snail draw portentously near. Burke pats the tank, reaches into a pocket and extracts an ancient lighter. Digging deeper, he pulls out a crumpled handkerchief. With a quick flick, he lights the lighter, and sets the handkerchief aflame.

He looks up at the monstrous snail. He smiles.

CONTINUES NEXT WEEK

RETRIBUTION
GAVIN CHAPPELL

'COME IN, Mr. Ray.'

He entered the white-walled room with something like terror clutching at him. Swallowing nervously, he blinked at the psychiatrist.

'Er... yes, yes of course,' Ray replied. Inwardly, he cursed. This wasn't like him.

'Now, if you'd lie down here, and tell me what you wanted to see me about.' The psychiatrist was a tall, thin, unhealthy man who carried himself in a manner part arrogant, part obsequious. As Ray sat down uncomfortably on the couch, two enormous eyes behind convex lensed glasses fixed him with a curious gaze.

'I believe you have suffered some kind of breakdown,' the psychiatrist prompted, glancing at his clipboard.

Ray frowned at him.

'Who told you that?' he demanded. 'Nonsense! I... I... it isn't true... I just...'

But as the psychiatrist silently returned his stare, Ray caught a hold of himself. He turned away.

After a minute or two, he began to speak.

'This must sound stupid,' he began. 'I am of the firm belief that'—he laughed nervously—'that a hitman is after me. Now, for a man in my position this is unlikely. The whole idea must sound like galloping paranoia to you, but... there it is.' He paused.

'Go on,' said the psychiatrist. 'Do you have any idea where this belief, this delusion, stems from?'

'Yes.' The patient swallowed. He concentrated on the wall in front of him.

'It began at school. I was in the fourth or fifth form... No, I'm wrong—it was the sixth form. In the first year of the sixth form I was re-sitting my exams, having made an unholy mess of them in the fifth form. This meant I had plenty of spare time for once. And it was during one of these free periods that it began.

'I forget precisely why, but for some reason I had been up on the first floor, and I was just heading down the stairs into the entrance hall. On the far side, a boy was standing, studying a noticeboard. He would have been beneath my notice normally, but something made me glance over at him. As I did so, he swung round and—well, he seemed to be pretending to aim a gun at me. A small, ginger-haired, thin young lad in a school uniform, for no apparent reason training an imaginary gun on me. I smiled, bemused, and walked across the hall to the far side, shaking my head as he swung round to keep his gun trained on me.' Ray stopped, his throat dry again.

The psychiatrist noticed sweat had broken out on his patient's fleshy brow. His face was white, and his hands were fumbling nervously at the sides of the couch.

'I appreciated the absurdity of it all, and treated it as no more than a weird schoolboy joke. At the time I was very pleased with my new-found maturity, and a little contemptuous of the lower school.

'So, I just laughed it off.

'A few days later, I was in the entrance hall again, at lunchtime. The hall bustled with schoolchildren buying snacks from the tuck-shop and being ushered outside by the prefects. I was chatting with another sixth former by the foot of the steps. I think we were looking out for someone, and that was why I turned round.

'The thin, ginger-haired boy was standing just behind me, with his imaginary gun.

'I just looked at him.

'My friend saw him too, and spoke rather condescendingly to him, asking him if he was going to shoot me. The boy said that he was a hitman, and he was going to shoot me, but he was waiting for some bullets. While this was going on, I just stood there, tongue-tied, amused by the weirdness of it, but also feeling—well, disturbed, I suppose.'

'And you see this as the root of your paranoia?' asked the psychiatrist, toying with an unlit cigarette. 'Did you have any other traumatic experiences at the time? Perhaps you may have forgotten them, or relegated them to the darker corners of your psyche.'

'This was the beginning of it,' Ray replied. 'But there's more.

'I stayed in the sixth form for a year, and all the while—about once a month—I'd see him, with his hands held as if he was training a gun on me. I used to worry about him, and I wondered if he had any friends.

'I could never speak to him; I suppose I was just struck dumb by the whole weirdness of it. Anyway, I secretly enjoyed it—it was just so bizarre.'

The psychiatrist lit up, filling the room with sweet smelling, expensive smoke.

'I this all you can tell me?' he asked.

'All? All? No, I told you—this was just the start.

'It was towards the end of the lower sixth that I began to believe that the boy was a ghost...' said Ray. His face was pale. The psychiatrist raised an eyebrow. Ray smiled, a little embarrassed. 'He was certainly haunting me,' he said. 'But I still couldn't work out why he'd picked on me. It was only then that I... I remembered the first year... Oh god.'

'Yes?'

'Oh, it was nothing,' said Ray dismissively. 'I got mixed up in some nonsense with Ouija boards, you know the sort of thing kids get up to. After a while, we became convinced that we'd summoned up the spirit of a former pupil, and the game began to get a bit serious—we were convinced that the boy wanted something, and we tried to provide it. There was one boy, a friend of mine, who was the real ringleader... But he was asked to leave the school in the end, and afterwards everything calmed down. We left the ghosts well alone, and gave them nothing.

'This was years before. It's probably irrelevant.' But the patient was shaking.

'But you feel there must be some kind of connection?'

'No, no, it was something I just remembered now. I don't know why.

'But the business with the kid continued until I left school. On the last day, I saw him again. This time, I spoke to him.

'I demanded to know why he kept on doing this, and he said.... "They're coming... The bullets... Someday soon, or maybe not so soon—but I'm going to finish you off one day, when you think you're on top of it all..." I just stared at him, then hurried off. By then I was starting to get pretty paranoid. But then I left, and got a job in the city, a lovely wife, and three equally lovely children.

'I am now thirty-four, and until a few days ago, I'd forgotten all about this.'

'Until a few days ago, you say.'

Ray took a deep breath.

'Could I have a glass of water, please?'

The psychiatrist nodded, and went to the sink. Filling a glass with water, he stared out of the window. It was getting dark.

He returned to the patient and handed him a glass. Ray

drank.

'I was out shopping,' he said suddenly, putting the glass down. 'I was with my wife. We were in the Precinct, just coming out of a shop. I heard something, I don't know what—a whispering? A rustling?—But it made me turn round. I could see nothing out of the ordinary, just someone standing there... But then I recognised him.'

'The boy?'

'The boy indeed! He hadn't changed! He was just the same as he'd been twenty years ago! He stood there in the middle of the deserted walkway, and although it was some way off, I could see that he was holding something.

'I became aware of my wife speaking to me, asking me what I was staring at. She couldn't see him. Then he turned and vanished round a corner.'

Ray was silent.

'So you decided to get help?' asked the psychiatrist.

Ray nodded.

'I remember now that when we all placed our hands on the glass in the circle of letters, I had heard a rustling that made me look over my shoulder for no reason—and it was then that I thought I saw the dark figure in the shadows. Then it happened again, when I first saw the boy! He's tracked me down after all these years, and he's going to kill me!'

'Calm down man! You're becoming irrational!' said the psychiatrist sharply, disturbed. In a few seconds the debonair, if slightly nervous, Mr. Ray had transformed into a frothing madman. At the psychiatrist's words, he sat back, calming.

There was a sound from outside, like the rustle of leaves.

'What was that?' Ray demanded. The psychiatrist shot a glance over his shoulder, towards the window.

'Nothing!' he said suddenly, laying a hand on him. 'J- just stay there... it's noth—nothing.' The stammer he had taken such pains to eradicate had returned. Nothing in his experience or his reading had prepared him for this.

'What is it?' Ray shouted. He tore away the psychiatrist's restraining hand, and leapt from the couch to stare....

At the window.

He was standing at the window, the ginger-haired boy, in his outdated school uniform. He was cradling something in his hands.

Ray froze, unable to move, as the boy pulled the trigger...

THE END.

THE JEWEL OF THE SEVEN STARS
BRAM STOKER

Chapter I: A Summons in the Night

IT ALL seemed so real that I could hardly imagine that it had ever occurred before; and yet each episode came, not as a fresh step in the logic of things, but as something expected. It is in such a wise that memory plays its pranks for good or ill; for pleasure or pain; for weal or woe. It is thus that life is bittersweet, and that which has been done becomes eternal.

Again, the light skiff, ceasing to shoot through the lazy water as when the oars flashed and dripped, glided out of the fierce July sunlight into the cool shade of the great drooping willow branches—I standing up in the swaying boat, she sitting still and with deft fingers guarding herself from stray twigs or the freedom of the resilience of moving boughs. Again, the water looked golden-brown under the canopy of translucent green; and the grassy bank was of emerald hue. Again, we sat in the cool shade, with the myriad noises of nature both without and within our bower merging into that drowsy hum in whose sufficing environment the great world with its disturbing trouble, and its more disturbing joys, can be effectually forgotten. Again, in that blissful solitude the young girl lost the convention of her prim, narrow upbringing, and told me in a natural, dreamy way of the loneliness of her new life. With an undertone of sadness she made me feel how in that spacious home each one of the household was isolated by the personal magnificence of her father and herself; that there confidence had no altar, and sympathy no shrine; and that there even her father's face was as distant as the old country life seemed now. Once more, the wisdom of my manhood and the experience of my years laid themselves at the girl's feet. It was seemingly their own doing; for the individual 'I' had no say in the matter, but only just obeyed imperative orders. And once again the flying seconds multiplied themselves endlessly. For it is in the arcana of dreams that existences merge and renew themselves, change and yet keep the same—like the soul of a musician in a fugue. And so memory swooned, again and again, in sleep.

It seems that there is never to be any perfect rest. Even in Eden the snake rears its head among the laden boughs of the Tree of Knowledge. The silence of the dreamless night is broken by the roar of the avalanche; the hissing of sudden floods; the clanging of the engine bell marking its sweep through a sleeping American town; the clanking of distant paddles over the sea.... Whatever it is, it is breaking the charm of my Eden. The canopy of greenery above us, starred with diamond-points of light, seems to quiver in the ceaseless beat of paddles; and the restless bell seems as though it would never cease....

All at once the gates of Sleep were thrown wide open, and my waking ears took in the cause of the disturbing sounds. Waking existence is prosaic enough—there was somebody knocking and ringing at someone's street door.

I was pretty well accustomed in my Jermyn Street

chambers to passing sounds; usually I did not concern myself, sleeping or waking, with the doings, however noisy, of my neighbours. But this noise was too continuous, too insistent, too imperative to be ignored. There was some active intelligence behind that ceaseless sound; and some stress or need behind the intelligence. I was not altogether selfish, and at the thought of someone's need I was, without premeditation, out of bed. Instinctively I looked at my watch. It was just three o'clock; there was a faint edging of grey round the green blind which darkened my room. It was evident that the knocking and ringing were at the door of our own house; and it was evident, too, that there was no one awake to answer the call. I slipped on my dressing-gown and slippers, and went down to the hall door. When I opened it there stood a dapper groom, with one hand pressed unflinchingly on the electric bell whilst with the other he raised a ceaseless clangour with the knocker. The instant he saw me the noise ceased; one hand went up instinctively to the brim of his hat, and the other produced a letter from his pocket. A neat brougham was opposite the door, the horses were breathing heavily as though they had come fast. A policeman, with his night lantern still alight at his belt, stood by, attracted to the spot by the noise.

'Beg pardon, sir, I'm sorry for disturbing you, but my orders was imperative; I was not to lose a moment, but to knock and ring till someone came. May I ask you, sir, if Mr. Malcolm Ross lives here?'

'I am Mr. Malcolm Ross.'

'Then this letter is for you, sir, and the bro'am is for you too, sir!'

I took, with a strange curiosity, the letter which he handed to me. As a barrister I had had, of course, odd experiences now and then, including sudden demands upon my time; but never anything like this. I stepped back into the hall, closing the door to, but leaving it ajar; then I switched on the electric light. The letter was directed in a strange hand, a woman's. It began at once without 'dear sir' or any such address:

'You said you would like to help me if I needed it; and I believe you meant what you said. The time has come sooner than I expected. I am in dreadful trouble, and do not know where to turn, or to whom to apply. An attempt has, I fear, been made to murder my Father; though, thank God, he still lives. But he is quite unconscious. The doctors and police have been sent for; but there is no one here whom I can depend on. Come at once if you are able to; and forgive me if you can. I suppose I shall realise later what I have done in asking such a favour; but at present I cannot think. Come! Come at once! MARGARET TRELAWNY.'

Pain and exultation struggled in my mind as I read; but the mastering thought was that she was in trouble and had called on me—me! My dreaming of her, then, was not altogether without a cause. I called out to the groom:

'Wait! I shall be with you in a minute!' Then I flew upstairs.

A very few minutes sufficed to wash and dress; and we were soon driving through the streets as fast as the horses could go. It was market morning, and when we got out on Piccadilly there was an endless stream of carts coming from the west; but for the rest the roadway was clear, and we went quickly. I had told the groom to come into the brougham with me so that he could tell me what had happened as we went along. He sat awkwardly, with his hat on his knees as he spoke.

'Miss Trelawny, sir, sent a man to tell us to get out a carriage at once; and when we was ready she come herself and gave me the letter and told Morgan—the coachman, sir—to fly. She said as I was to lose not a second, but to keep knocking till someone come.'

'Yes, I know, I know—you told me! What I want to know is, why she sent for me. What happened in the house?'

'I don't quite know myself, sir; except that master was found in his room senseless, with the sheets all bloody, and a wound on his head. He couldn't be waked nohow. 'Twas Miss Trelawny herself as found him.'

'How did she come to find him at such an hour? It was late in the night, I suppose?'

'I don't know, sir; I didn't hear nothing at all of the details.'

As he could tell me no more, I stopped the carriage for a moment to let him get out on the box; then I turned the matter over in my mind as I sat alone. There were many things which I could have asked the servant; and for a few moments after he had gone I was angry with myself for not having used my opportunity. On second thought, however, I was glad the temptation was gone. I felt that it would be more delicate to learn what I wanted to know of Miss Trelawny's surroundings from herself, rather than from her servants.

We bowled swiftly along Knightsbridge, the small noise of our well-appointed vehicle sounding hollowly in the morning air. We turned up the Kensington Palace Road and presently stopped opposite a great house on the left-hand side, nearer, so far as I could judge, the Notting Hill than the Kensington end of the avenue. It was a truly fine house, not only with regard to size but to architecture. Even in the dim grey light of the morning, which tends to diminish the size of things, it looked big.

Miss Trelawny met me in the hall. She was not in any way shy. She seemed to rule all around her with a sort of high-bred dominance, all the more remarkable as she was greatly agitated and as pale as snow. In the great hall were several servants, the men standing together near the hall door, and the women clinging together in the further corners and doorways. A police superintendent had been talking to Miss Trelawny; two men in uniform and one plain-clothes man stood near him. As she took my hand impulsively there was a look of relief in her eyes, and she gave a gentle sigh of relief. Her salutation was simple.

'I knew you would come!'

The clasp of the hand can mean a great deal, even when it is not intended to mean anything especially. Miss Trelawny's hand somehow became lost in my own. It was not that it was a small hand; it was fine and flexible, with long delicate fingers—a rare and beautiful hand; it was the unconscious self-surrender. And though at the moment I could not dwell on the cause of the thrill which swept me, it came back to me later.

She turned and said to the police superintendent:

'This is Mr. Malcolm Ross.' The police officer saluted as he answered:

'I know Mr. Malcolm Ross, miss. Perhaps he will remember I had the honour of working with him in the Brixton Coining case.' I had not at first glance noticed who it was, my whole attention having been taken with Miss Trelawny.

'Of course, Superintendent Dolan, I remember very well!' I said as we shook hands. I could not but note that the acquaintanceship seemed a relief to Miss Trelawny. There was a certain vague uneasiness in her manner which took my attention; instinctively I felt that it would be less embarrassing for her to speak with me alone. So I said to the Superintendent:

'Perhaps it will be better if Miss Trelawny will see me alone for a few minutes. You, of course, have already heard all she knows; and I shall understand better how things are if I may ask some questions. I will then talk the matter over with you if I may.'

'I shall be glad to be of what service I can, sir,' he answered heartily.

Following Miss Trelawny, I moved over to a dainty room which opened from the hall and looked out on the garden at the back of the house. When we had entered and I had closed the door she said:

'I will thank you later for your goodness in coming to

me in my trouble; but at present you can best help me when you know the facts.'

'Go on,' I said. 'Tell me all you know and spare no detail, however trivial it may at the present time seem to be.' She went on at once:

'I was awakened by some sound; I do not know what. I only know that it came through my sleep; for all at once I found myself awake, with my heart beating wildly, listening anxiously for some sound from my Father's room. My room is next Father's, and I can often hear him moving about before I fall asleep. He works late at night, sometimes very late indeed; so that when I wake early, as I do occasionally, or in the grey of the dawn, I hear him still moving. I tried once to remonstrate with him about staying up so late, as it cannot be good for him; but I never ventured to repeat the experiment. You know how stern and cold he can be—at least you may remember what I told you about him; and when he is polite in this mood he is dreadful. When he is angry I can bear it much better; but when he is slow and deliberate, and the side of his mouth lifts up to show the sharp teeth, I think I feel—well, I don't know how! Last night I got up softly and stole to the door, for I really feared to disturb him. There was not any noise of moving, and no kind of cry at all; but there was a queer kind of dragging sound, and a slow, heavy breathing. Oh! It was dreadful, waiting there in the dark and the silence, and fearing—fearing I did not know what!

'At last I took my courage a deux mains, and turning the handle as softly as I could, I opened the door a tiny bit. It was quite dark within; I could just see the outline of the windows. But in the darkness the sound of breathing, becoming more distinct, was appalling. As I listened, this continued; but there was no other sound. I pushed the door open all at once. I was afraid to open it slowly; I felt as if there might be some dreadful thing behind it ready to pounce out on me! Then I switched on the electric light, and stepped into the room. I looked first at the bed. The sheets were all crumpled up, so that I knew Father had been in bed; but there was a great dark red patch in the centre of the bed, and spreading to the edge of it, that made my heart stand still. As I was gazing at it the sound of the breathing came across the room, and my eyes followed to it. There was Father on his right side with the other arm under him, just as if his dead body had been thrown there all in a heap. The track of blood went across the room up to the bed, and there was a pool all around him which looked terribly red and glittering as I bent over to examine him. The place where he lay was right in front of the big safe. He was in his pyjamas. The left sleeve was torn, showing his bare arm, and stretched out toward the safe. It looked—oh! so terrible, patched all with blood, and with the flesh torn or cut all around a gold chain bangle on his wrist. I did not know he wore such a thing, and it seemed to give me a new shock of surprise.'

She paused a moment; and as I wished to relieve her by a moment's divergence of thought, I said:

'Oh, that need not surprise you. You will see the most unlikely men wearing bangles. I have seen a judge condemn a man to death, and the wrist of the hand he held up had a gold bangle.' She did not seem to heed much the words or the idea; the pause, however, relieved her somewhat, and she went on in a steadier voice:

'I did not lose a moment in summoning aid, for I feared he might bleed to death. I rang the bell, and then went out and called for help as loudly as I could. In what must have been a very short time—though it seemed an incredibly long one to me—some of the servants came running up; and then others, till the room seemed full of staring eyes, and dishevelled hair, and night clothes of all sorts.

'We lifted Father on a sofa; and the housekeeper, Mrs. Grant, who seemed to have her wits about her more than any of us, began to look where the flow of blood came from. In a few seconds it became apparent that it came from the arm which was bare. There was a deep wound—not clean-cut as with a knife, but like a jagged rent or tear—close to the wrist, which seemed to have cut into the vein. Mrs. Grant tied a handkerchief round the cut, and screwed it up tight with a silver paper-cutter; and the flow of blood seemed to be checked at once. By this time I had come to my senses—or such of them as remained; and I sent off one man for the doctor and another for the police. When they had gone, I felt that, except for the servants, I was all alone in the house, and that I knew nothing—of my Father or anything else; and a great longing came to me to have someone with me who could help me. Then I thought of you and your kind offer in the boat under the willow-tree; and, without waiting to think, I told the men to get a carriage ready at once, and I scribbled a note and sent it on to you.'

She paused. I did not like to say just then anything of how I felt. I looked at her; I think she understood, for her eyes were raised to mine for a moment and then fell, leaving her cheeks as red as peony roses. With a manifest effort she went on with her story:

'The Doctor was with us in an incredibly short time. The groom had met him letting himself into his house with his latchkey, and he came here running. He made a proper tourniquet for poor Father's arm, and then went home to get some appliances. I dare say he will be back almost immediately. Then a policeman came, and sent a message to the station; and very soon the Superintendent was here. Then you came.'

There was a long pause, and I ventured to take her hand for an instant. Without a word more we opened the door, and joined the Superintendent in the hall. He hurried up to us, saying as he came:

'I have been examining everything myself, and have sent off a message to Scotland Yard. You see, Mr. Ross, there seemed so much that was odd about the case that I thought we had better have the best man of the Criminal

Investigation Department that we could get. So I sent a note asking to have Sergeant Daw sent at once. You remember him, sir, in that American poisoning case at Hoxton.'

'Oh yes,' I said, 'I remember him well; in that and other cases, for I have benefited several times by his skill and acumen. He has a mind that works as truly as any that I know. When I have been for the defence, and believed my man was innocent, I was glad to have him against us!'

'That is high praise, sir!' said the Superintendent gratified: 'I am glad you approve of my choice; that I did well in sending for him.'

I answered heartily:

'Could not be better. I do not doubt that between you we shall get at the facts—and what lies behind them!'

We ascended to Mr. Trelawny's room, where we found everything exactly as his daughter had described.

There came a ring at the house bell, and a minute later a man was shown into the room. A young man with aquiline features, keen grey eyes, and a forehead that stood out square and broad as that of a thinker. In his hand he had a black bag which he at once opened. Miss Trelawny introduced us: 'Doctor Winchester, Mr. Ross, Superintendent Dolan.' We bowed mutually, and he, without a moment's delay, began his work. We all waited, and eagerly watched him as he proceeded to dress the wound. As he went on he turned now and again to call the Superintendent's attention to some point about the wound, the latter proceeding to enter the fact at once in his notebook.

'See! Several parallel cuts or scratches beginning on the left side of the wrist and in some places endangering the radial artery.

'These small wounds here, deep and jagged, seem as if made with a blunt instrument. This in particular would seem as if made with some kind of sharp wedge; the flesh round it seems torn as if with lateral pressure.'

Turning to Miss Trelawny he said presently:

'Do you think we might remove this bangle? It is not absolutely necessary, as it will fall lower on the wrist where it can hang loosely; but it might add to the patient's comfort later on.' The poor girl flushed deeply as she answered in a low voice:

'I do not know. I—I have only recently come to live with my Father; and I know so little of his life or his ideas that I fear I can hardly judge in such a matter. The Doctor, after a keen glance at her, said in a very kindly way:

'Forgive me! I did not know. But in any case you need not be distressed. It is not required at present to move it. Were it so I should do so at once on my own responsibility. If it be necessary later on, we can easily remove it with a file. Your Father doubtless has some object in keeping it as it is. See! There is a tiny key attached to it....' As he was speaking he stopped and bent lower, taking from my hand the candle which I held and lowering it till its light fell on the bangle. Then motioning me to hold the candle in the same position, he took from his pocket a magnifying-glass which he adjusted. When he had made a careful examination he stood up and handed the magnifying-glass to Dolan, saying as he did so:

'You had better examine it yourself. That is no ordinary bangle. The gold is wrought over triple steel links; see where it is worn away. It is manifestly not meant to be removed lightly; and it would need more than an ordinary file to do it.'

The Superintendent bent his great body; but not getting close enough that way knelt down by the sofa as the Doctor had done. He examined the bangle minutely, turning it slowly round so that no particle of it escaped observation. Then he stood up and handed the magnifying-glass to me. 'When you have examined it yourself,' he said, 'let the lady look at it if she will,' and he commenced to write at length in his notebook.

I made a simple alteration in his suggestion. I held out

the glass toward Miss Trelawny, saying:

'Had you not better examine it first?' She drew back, slightly raising her hand in disclaimer, as she said impulsively:

'Oh no! Father would doubtless have shown it to me had he wished me to see it. I would not like to without his consent.' Then she added, doubtless fearing lest her delicacy of view should give offence to the rest of us:

'Of course it is right that you should see it. You have to examine and consider everything; and indeed—indeed I am grateful to you...'

She turned away; I could see that she was crying quietly. It was evident to me that even in the midst of her trouble and anxiety there was a chagrin that she knew so little of her father; and that her ignorance had to be shown at such a time and amongst so many strangers. That they were all men did not make the shame more easy to bear, though there was a certain relief in it. Trying to interpret her feelings I could not but think that she must have been glad that no woman's eyes—of understanding greater than man's—were upon her in that hour.

When I stood up from my examination, which verified to me that of the Doctor, the latter resumed his place beside the couch and went on with his ministrations. Superintendent Dolan said to me in a whisper:

'I think we are fortunate in our doctor!' I nodded, and was about to add something in praise of his acumen, when there came a low tapping at the door.

CONTINUES NEXT WEEK.

A CONNECTICUT YANKEE IN KING ARTHUR'S COURT
MARK TWAIN

After being knocked on the head by an employee, the Connecticut Yankee has awoken to find himself in a land where he is accosted by an armoured knight. Assuming the man is a lunatic, the Yankee journeys on to a fair city called Camelot.

No read on...

Chapter II: King Arthur's Court

THE MOMENT I got a chance I slipped aside privately and touched an ancient common looking man on the shoulder and said, in an insinuating, confidential way:

'Friend, do me a kindness. Do you belong to the asylum, or are you just on a visit or something like that?'

He looked me over stupidly, and said:

'Marry, fair sir, me seemeth—'

'That will do,' I said; 'I reckon you are a patient.'

I moved away, cogitating, and at the same time keeping

an eye out for any chance passenger in his right mind that might come along and give me some light. I judged I had found one, presently; so I drew him aside and said in his ear:

'If I could see the head keeper a minute—only just a minute—'

'Prithee do not let me.'

'Let you what?'

'Hinder me, then, if the word please thee better. Then he went on to say he was an under-cook and could not stop to gossip, though he would like it another time; for it would comfort his very liver to know where I got my clothes. As he started away he pointed and said yonder was one who was idle enough for my purpose, and was seeking me besides, no doubt. This was an airy slim boy in shrimp-coloured tights that made him look like a forked carrot, the rest of his gear was blue silk and dainty laces and ruffles; and he had long yellow curls, and wore a plumed pink satin cap tilted complacently over his ear. By his look, he was good-natured; by his gait, he was satisfied with himself. He was pretty enough to frame. He arrived, looked me over with a smiling and impudent curiosity; said he had come for me, and informed me that he was a page.

'Go 'long,' I said; 'you ain't more than a paragraph.'

It was pretty severe, but I was nettled. However, it never fazed him; he didn't appear to know he was hurt. He began to talk and laugh, in happy, thoughtless, boyish fashion, as we walked along, and made himself old friends with me at once; asked me all sorts of questions about myself and about my clothes, but never waited for an answer—always chattered straight ahead, as if he didn't know he had asked a question and wasn't expecting any reply, until at last he happened to mention that he was born in the beginning of the year 513.

It made the cold chills creep over me! I stopped and said, a little faintly:

'Maybe I didn't hear you just right. Say it again—and

say it slow. What year was it?'

'513.'

'513! You don't look it! Come, my boy, I am a stranger and friendless; be honest and honourable with me. Are you in your right mind?'

He said he was.

'Are these other people in their right minds?'

He said they were.

'And this isn't an asylum? I mean, it isn't a place where they cure crazy people?'

He said it wasn't.

'Well, then,' I said, 'either I am a lunatic, or something just as awful has happened. Now tell me, honest and true, where am I?'

'IN KING ARTHUR'S COURT.'

I waited a minute, to let that idea shudder its way home, and then said:

'And according to your notions, what year is it now?'

'528—nineteenth of June.'

I felt a mournful sinking at the heart, and muttered: 'I shall never see my friends again—never, never again. They will not be born for more than thirteen hundred years yet.'

I seemed to believe the boy, I didn't know why. Something in me seemed to believe him—my consciousness, as you may say; but my reason didn't. My reason straightway began to clamour; that was natural. I didn't know how to go about satisfying it, because I knew that the testimony of men wouldn't serve—my reason would say they were lunatics, and throw out their evidence. But all of a sudden I stumbled on the very thing, just by luck. I knew that the only total eclipse of the sun in the first half of the sixth century occurred on the 21st of June, A.D. 528, O.S., and began at 3 minutes after 12 noon. I also knew that no total eclipse of the sun was due in what to me was the present year—i.e., 1879. So, if I could keep my anxiety and curiosity from eating the heart out of me for forty-eight hours, I should then find out for certain whether this boy was telling me the truth or not.

Wherefore, being a practical Connecticut man, I now shoved this whole problem clear out of my mind till its appointed day and hour should come, in order that I might turn all my attention to the circumstances of the present moment, and be alert and ready to make the most out of them that could be made. One thing at a time, is my motto—and just play that thing for all it is worth, even if it's only two pair and a jack. I made up my mind to two things: if it was still the nineteenth century and I was among lunatics and couldn't get away, I would presently boss that asylum or know the reason why; and if, on the other hand, it was really the sixth century, all right, I didn't want any softer thing: I would boss the whole country inside of three months; for I judged I would have the start of the best-educated man in the kingdom by a matter of thirteen hundred years and upward. I'm not a man to waste time after my mind's made up and there's work on hand; so I said to the page:

'Now, Clarence, my boy—if that might happen to be your name—I'll get you to post me up a little if you don't mind. What is the name of that apparition that brought me here?'

'My master and thine? That is the good knight and great lord Sir Kay the Seneschal, foster brother to our liege the king.'

'Very good; go on, tell me everything.'

He made a long story of it; but the part that had immediate interest for me was this: He said I was Sir Kay's prisoner, and that in the due course of custom I would be flung into a dungeon and left there on scant commons until my friends ransomed me—unless I chanced to rot, first. I saw that the last chance had the best show, but I didn't waste any bother about that; time was too precious. The page said, further, that dinner was about ended in the great hall by this time, and that as soon as the sociability and the heavy drinking should begin, Sir Kay would have me in and exhibit me before King Arthur and his illustrious knights seated at the Table Round, and would brag about his exploit in capturing me, and would probably exaggerate the facts a little, but it wouldn't be good form for me to correct him, and not over safe, either; and when I was done being exhibited, then ho for the dungeon; but he, Clarence, would find a way to come and see me every now and then, and cheer me up, and help me get word to my friends.

Get word to my friends! I thanked him; I couldn't do less; and about this time a lackey came to say I was wanted; so Clarence led me in and took me off to one side and sat down by me.

Well, it was a curious kind of spectacle, and interesting. It was an immense place, and rather naked—yes, and full of loud contrasts. It was very, very lofty; so lofty that the banners depending from the arched beams and girders away up there floated in a sort of twilight; there was a stone-railed gallery at each end, high up, with musicians in the one, and women, clothed in stunning colours, in the other. The floor was of big stone flags laid in black and white squares, rather battered by age and use, and needing repair. As to ornament, there wasn't any, strictly speaking; though on the walls hung some huge tapestries which were probably taxed as works of art; battle-pieces, they were, with horses shaped like those which children cut out of paper or create in gingerbread; with men on them in scale armour whose scales are represented by round holes—so that the man's coat looks as if it had been done with a biscuit-punch. There was a fireplace big enough to camp in; and its projecting sides and hood, of carved and pillared stonework, had the look of a cathedral door. Along the walls stood men-at-arms, in breastplate and morion, with halberds for their only weapon—rigid as statues; and that is what they looked like.

In the middle of this groined and vaulted public square was an oaken table which they called the Table Round. It was as large as a circus ring; and around it sat a great company of men dressed in such various and splendid colours that it hurt one's eyes to look at them. They wore their plumed hats, right along, except that whenever one addressed himself directly to the king, he lifted his hat a trifle just as he was beginning his remark.

Mainly they were drinking—from entire ox horns; but a few were still munching bread or gnawing beef bones. There was about an average of two dogs to one man; and these sat in expectant attitudes till a spent bone was flung to them, and then they went for it by brigades and divisions, with a rush, and there ensued a fight which filled the prospect with a tumultuous chaos of plunging heads and bodies and flashing tails, and the storm of howlings and barkings deafened all speech for the time; but that was no matter, for the dog-fight was always a bigger interest anyway; the men rose, sometimes, to observe it the better and bet on it, and the ladies and the musicians stretched themselves out over their balusters with the same object; and all broke into delighted ejaculations from time to time. In the end, the winning dog stretched himself out comfortably with his bone between his paws, and proceeded to growl over it, and gnaw it, and grease the floor with it, just as fifty others were already doing; and the rest of the court resumed their previous industries and entertainments.

As a rule, the speech and behaviour of these people were gracious and courtly; and I noticed that they were good and serious listeners when anybody was telling anything—I mean in a dog-fightless interval. And plainly, too, they were a childlike and innocent lot; telling lies of the stateliest pattern with a most gentle and winning naivety, and ready and willing to listen to anybody else's lie, and believe it, too. It was hard to associate them with anything cruel or dreadful; and yet they dealt in tales of blood and suffering with a guileless relish that made me almost forget to shudder.

I was not the only prisoner present. There were twenty or more. Poor devils, many of them were maimed, hacked, carved, in a frightful way; and their hair, their faces, their clothing, were caked with black and stiffened drenchings of blood. They were suffering sharp physical pain, of course; and weariness, and hunger and thirst, no doubt; and at least none had given them the comfort of a wash, or even the poor charity of a lotion for their wounds; yet you never heard them utter a moan or a groan, or saw them show any sign of restlessness, or any disposition to complain. The thought was forced upon me: 'The rascals—they have served other people so in their day; it being their own turn, now, they were not expecting any better treatment than this; so their philosophical bearing is not an outcome of mental training, intellectual fortitude, reasoning; it is mere animal training; they are white Indians.'

CONTINUES NEXT WEEK

Made in the USA
Columbia, SC
07 April 2022